For Jude

Melvin Burgess

LADY

My life as a bitch

Andersen Press • London

First published in 2001 by
Andersen Press Limited,
20 Vauxhall Bridge Road, London SW1V 2SA
www.andersenpress.co.uk

British Library Cataloguing in Publication Data available
ISBN 0 86264 770 3

Typeset in 12/15pt Perpetua by FiSH Books, London WC1
Printed and bound in Great Britain by
Mackays of Chatham Ltd., Chatham, Kent

ONE

It was me and Wayne heading down Copson Street. Michelle and Dobby were there too, trailing behind. They were jealous, both of them. She fancied Wayne and Dobby fancied me, but it was me and Wayne, me and Wayne, me and Wayne all morning. He was leaning over and smiling, tickling me and touching me. I wasn't going to say no, was I?

We'd been trying to lose them for the past hour, but we hadn't really got off with each other yet, so we couldn't just push off. I knew what was going on between us right from the first but I think it had just been occurring to him as we went along. We were outside Somerfield's and Michelle and Dobby had dropped back outside the baker's when he reached forward and tickled the palm of my hand. It sent little shivers up my arm. My hand closed around his and we gave one another a little squeeze, and that was it. We were holding hands. We turned and looked into each other's faces and . . .

I was just thrilled. You know? That moment. I just love that moment. I could do it over and over again until the end of my life. I mean, all right, he wasn't the

1

first boy ever, or even the first boy that month. In fact, the way I was then he'd have been pretty lucky if he was the first one that week. But still — it just made me shine. There was the sunshine sparkling on the wet pavements. There were the people and the shops, there was Dobbs fancying me and Michelle all jealous because she wanted what I had, and there was Wayne smiling down at me, all pleased and happy because I was holding his hand. He was gorgeous. I was gorgeous. Isn't that just about the nicest thing you can think of?

He leaned down to my ear and whispered, 'Let's go.'

'Where do you want to go?' I asked. I glanced back. Michelle had walked up near to us and she was standing there looking daggers.

'In your knickers,' said Wayne and I said,

'Ooh, yeah.' He looked surprised. He bent close to me and whispered in my ear,

'You're making my head go.'

I grinned. He was lovely, he was mine. He put his arms round me and he sort of snuffled in my ear. I giggled. It made me tingle all over, but I was bothered about Michelle. I looked over his shoulder at her. 'I'll talk to you later,' I mouthed, but she pulled a face and looked away. I suppose I should've said something to her before. I was making a mess of things, really. It was a pity in some ways because I thought we might all be friends, and I mean, you can get on and off with the boys in a crowd, but if you fall out with the girls, you're out. It made me angry with myself, because I'd been through enough friends recently. But I knew I wasn't going to stop myself.

I'd been off my head lately. And it'd been great, you know? Really, really great. The best time I'd ever had. Only, I was getting fed up. Well, not fed up — tired. It'd been going on a long time. It'd been a lot of boys and a lot of late nights and a lot of voddies and a lot of Red Bulls and a lot of e. That crowd, Michelle and Dobby, even Wayne — they weren't me. I'd even been thinking, maybe I'd give my old friends a ring. Annie. That crowd. They'd still be there.

But Wayne made me forget all that. I wanted him. And I was going to have him.

We ran off round behind Somerfield's into the car park. I was giggling. I was thinking, Here I go again! Michelle and Dobby stared after us but they didn't try to follow. We ran through the car park and onto the road behind it. We got round behind the wall and Wayne stopped and turned to face me and we put our arms round each other and we kissed. It was a funny kiss because we were both out of breath as well as being turned on, but after it was done we both let out a long sigh and pulled each other close. What a relief!

'I've been wanting to do that all morning,' groaned Wayne. I glanced round, but the others were well gone. I relaxed. He reached for my mouth again and this time the kiss went right through me. I made a little 'oh, oh,' noise, and that turned him on even more. I hung onto his neck and held up my face and ground myself right into him.

'Jesus,' said Wayne. He slid his hands under my top and down the side of my bra. His hands were lovely and warm. I was underdressed as usual. 'Where can we go?' he asked, looking around as if a bed was going to spring out of the ground.

'There's nowhere to go,' I said, and I laughed because – I dunno. Like I say, there'd been all these boys lately. Everyone had been saying it. Annie, my best friend at school had said it, my mum had said it, my sister Julie had said it. 'All those boys!' I'd wanted them all so much but now, somehow, I was kind of pleased that there was nowhere to go. It was like, poor old Wayne, just his luck! I'd have shagged him up against the wall for a bag of jelly beans a month ago but times were changing.

Well, maybe they were.

I slid out from under him and ran off, laughing at him. I was twisting round to look at him and that's why I ran into the alchie.

He was standing on the pavement right in front of me with a can of Special Brew in his hand. I banged right into him, full on. I thought maybe he was going to get nasty but he smiled and touched me gently on my hip.

'Steady, steady,' he said.

I smiled back because...well, because I was it, wasn't I? No wonder Michelle was jealous! Wayne fancied me like anything. Dobby fancied me – I knew that, the way he looked at me, although he never said. And now even this alchie. I could see him glancing down at me, and I expect he was jealous of me as well, because I had everything and he nothing. All right, he was just a tramp, he wasn't going to get anywhere near me. But still. I want everyone to fancy me. Not just the sports stars and the pop stars and all the boys. I'd like the old men and the young men and everyone to fancy me. I'd like the money in your pocket and the dirt on your shoe to turn round and look at me when I go past.

Then I thought, What's he doing? And I stepped back quick – what right did he have to touch me? Just because I banged into him? Wayne didn't like it either. He said, 'Keep your hands off,' in a sharp voice, and I said,

'*Excuse* me!'

'Why, what have you done?' said the alchie, and he gave me this shitty little smile.

I'd seen him around. I'd seen him on the bench by the flowershop near the telephone booths drinking with old blokes, and I'd seen him sitting in a blanket on a piece of cardboard with a dog on a piece of string at the other end of Copson Street, begging for change. He never even got it together to sell the *Big Issue*. He wasn't old, he was a young man. You'd think he hadn't had time to get worn down. He was still good looking under the dirt and the booze. He looked strong. He had nice hair, he had a good face. But...

'You're just an alcoholic,' said Wayne, and I said, 'Yeah!'

He gave us this crooked look. 'Give me a quid and

I'll leave you alone,' he said. He said it like it was half a joke.

'I'm not giving you anything,' said Wayne.

The alchie glared at us. Maybe he was just being friendly, but he shouldn't have touched me. Then he nodded at me and said, spitefully, 'And your girlfriend's a slut, so what?'

'Get lost!' I yelled. That just made me so angry. So angry! Calling me names like that. I lashed out and knocked his can of Special Brew out of his hand. I didn't mean to. I was just fed up suddenly. I was fed up with things going all wrong. I mean! Everything could have been just right so easily. Everyone fancied me. I had Wayne there with his tongue practically hitting the floor. I should have been smiling my head off! But instead I had Michelle pulling faces at me and now this drunk. I mean, why do things work out like that? I could have fancied someone else, or Michelle might have been decent about it and understood, and the drunk could've been — I dunno, somewhere else. But it had to be shitty, didn't it? It had to be. It just seemed like everything I wanted to do lately had to go wrong because of other people.

I caught the can just right. It flew out of his hand and banged onto the ground. There was this horrible silence before my whole life vanished.

He was furious, you could see it in his face. He wasn't all that tall, Wayne was taller, but the alchie was a grown man and Wayne took a step back. 'My drink!'

he squeaked as it fell. The beer spurted out onto the road and he scrabbled on his knees to get it before it all went. He got up and stood there shaking the can by his ear, slowly realising that there was nothing left. Then he got furious.

'My bitch, you little drink. My bitch!' he yelled. He was so angry about a little drink of beer. Wayne started laughing, because he got bitch and drink mixed up, but then he lifted his hand to grab me and I had to step back quick.

'Sorry!' I gasped. But he kept coming at me. He was falling on top of me. I had to run backwards. It was amazing – him so upset about a can of beer. He was about ready to pull my head off, I could tell by his face – it was all twisted up with rage and hate and horrible things. I was running backwards and he was still coming, so I had to twist round and leap away. Then I looked back but he was *still* right there, right there with his hands on my clothes. It gave me a fright but I still thought then that I could get away with a few steps.

'Wayne!' I shouted. I ran a few fast steps and looked round, but even before my head turned I could hear his breath right in my ear and that's when I started to get really scared because he just kept coming.

Something strange was happening. Everything around us seemed to be frozen. I was having to run really fast. I was thinking, The police station is just around the corner. I bombed up through the car park and onto Copson Street and then onto Hill Street by the police station. I could have opened the door and got in, but the bloody place was only closed, wasn't it? I forgot, they shut it down a couple of weeks ago. I just had time to grab the door and tug and scream and then run off. I could feel his fingers in my hair – I swear he was that close. I didn't dare stop. I was screaming at people to help me but, funny thing, everyone just watched me go. They didn't seem concerned, they just looked mildly surprised.

He was yelling something at me, but he was getting all wheezy already. I'm amazed he made it that far. I ran round the corner and behind the shops. He was on my back the whole time. I was terrified. Why wasn't anyone stopping him? None of it made any sense. Then I was round behind the café. There was the smell of grease and dustbins and before I knew it, I was falling over the bins. I was on my hands and knees. I rolled over in the rubbish and there he was, still right on me, staring down.

I screamed, 'Leave me alone!'

He looked at me, he licked his lips and he glanced over his shoulder and back at me. I knew what he was thinking. We were on our own. It was crazy. It was Saturday, it was the middle of the day, but somehow we were on our own. He couldn't rape me but he could pull my clothes about and feel me up and get angry with me if he wanted.

'You little bitch!' he yelled, so full of anger I was terrified.

'Get away! You bastard!' I screamed. I was looking around for Wayne and the others but they weren't there. Why weren't they there? He smiled at me again and stepped closer. I got back on all fours facing him and bared my teeth at him.

As I watched him, his face changed into pure shock.

'Oh, God, no. I'm sorry, I'm sorry,' he said. Actually he more or less screamed it. He was backing off with his hands up near his face as if I was going to do something to him.

'You're for it, you're dead,' I told him. I was trying to stand up but I couldn't.

'No, oh God, no! I didn't mean this to happen, please! Oh, Jesus Lord, not again!' he said. He looked awful, really upset. I couldn't help myself. I jumped forward and bit his hand. I bit it! 'Get off me!' he yelled. He stumbled backwards and fell over. I was off. I didn't have any trouble leaving him behind this time. I jumped clean over him and I was away. I've never run so fast. I didn't pause to look for Wayne and the others. I was so scared I ran straight back home, yelping, 'Mum! Mum! Mum!' as I went. And all the time I was thinking – I bit him? I couldn't believe I'd bitten him.

The running was so good. I didn't know why, I never liked to run. Even though I was scared I had this big thrill about going so fast and even after I knew the tramp was miles away, I still kept running and running and I couldn't understand how it was I wasn't out of breath.

All around me the world was changing. The cars, the dustbins, the grass, the dog shit on the tarmac, the feet that had been and gone – everything left its taste on my tongue. Things were crowding into my mouth and my nose. At the same time, everything I could see was moving further away and growing tall and slow at the same time. The world was changing shape, growing in one direction, closing down in others. I was in one weird state! As I came haring round by Yew Tree Road and turned into the estate, I remember thinking, It must be fear's done this to me. My house was only fifty metres away, about two seconds at my speed, and I started howling and barking, 'Mum! Mum! Mum!' at the top of my voice as I got close. I jumped right over the little brick wall at our front and ran round the back and in the door. Mum was in the kitchen.

'God Jesus!' she yelled as I came in.

'Mum, Mum, Mum, I've had this terrible scare, Mum,' I shouted, and I flung myself at her.

Mum screamed and I stopped in my tracks. She looked terrified! I've never seen such a look on her face. 'Get away!' she screamed. 'Back! Back! Shoo!' She reached out and grabbed hold of the frying pan and flung it at me. I just stood there, I was like a dummy, I watched the oil spilling out in a silver flash and then the pan caught me right on the side of my face.

'Ow! Ah! Mum, what for? What's wrong?' I shouted, but she'd gone mad. She was crawling backwards onto the work surface, getting her feet off the ground and staring at me with that terrible, mad face.

'Get away!' she screamed again, and her hand was

groping along the work surface for something else to chuck at me. I took a few steps forwards, shaking my head, which really hurt. I only wanted a cuddle! I put my arms out and fell onto my nose.

'It's mad!' she shouted. And she started banging on the window shouting, 'Mad dog! Mad dog! Help!'

She'd gone hysterical. I ran out of the room to get help just in time to see my brother Adam come down the stairs. I started to ask what was wrong with Mum, but I could see by his face that he was scared, too.

'Stay away, get back, Adam. It's a mad dog, it might have rabies or something,' Mum yelled. I thought...Dog? Rabies? What? Adam turned and ran up the stairs, and then it clicked. I realised – there must be a mad dog in the house! I looked around and I couldn't see it anywhere, but it had to be right there because Mum was staring straight at me. She looked at me like it was *clinging* to me. I was terrified but at the same time I was just devastated. In an emergency like this, Mum was showing what she really thought and felt about me. I mean, there she was shouting desperately at Adam to get away, but she couldn't spare the time to even say my name, and the thing must be almost at my feet. I thought – *at my feet*! I screamed and jumped about ten feet in the air and ran up the stairs after Adam.

'Run, run,' I barked and Mum screeched, 'Run, Adam!' His room was nearest, and you know what? The bastard slammed the door in my face. Can you believe that – a mad dog on the stairs and he slammed the door in my face!

11

'Adam, no!' I howled, but all he did was bellow,
'Go away! Go away! Bad dog!'

I ran to my own room. I couldn't see the dog anywhere – it was terrifying, like it was invisible or something. I pushed the door open and sprang in. I spun round and tried to lock the door but, you know what? I couldn't do it. It was so weird. I was fumbling with the handle and I suddenly realised, no wonder I couldn't close it, I was trying to do it with my mouth. There was this awful, weird moment when I was hanging there from the handle with my mouth, thinking . . . What am I *doing*? Then I dropped to the ground and jumped up onto my dressing table out of the way and there was the dog on there with me.

Yeah, well. I could say that. I could say I thought that, but I knew at once. I think I knew already, sort of, and that's why I jumped up, to have a look in the mirror. I didn't think that reflection was anyone else's but mine, not for one second. The dog was one of those scruffy black and white mongrel things with a stupid face and twitchy ears and it was me. It all fell into place – the way I'd run so fast, the smells, the way I bit the tramp, my mum and Adam getting so scared of me. It was obvious, but it was so crazy my mind was going bonkers trying to find ways of thinking it wasn't true, because who wants to think that? Who *could* think that? How could it be true?

I barked in fright and the dog barked back, and I think I might have fainted then, because there I was on the floor rolling about, shaking my head and growling. Then I tried to stand up. I'd just *known* there was something funny about my posture. I made a real effort to get up on two legs but I fell straight down. I did it about three times, but I just fell down — one, two, three. Then I sat there trying to talk and listening to what was coming out of my mouth.

'Wow! Wow! Wow!' I said. 'Wow! Wow-wow-wow-wow! Agrrrr.' And that was it.

My door slammed with a violent thud that made my ears pop.

'It's trapped, it's trapped, I've trapped it in Sandra's room,' shouted Adam triumphantly.

I went, 'Ah!' like you do when something stupid's happened, and this time it sounded just like me because I wasn't using my tongue.

'Good boy!' Mum was at the bottom of the stairs. I could hear her panting. I held my breath to hear what they were going to do next.

'I'll call the police,' she said. 'Jesus, it came right at me. If I hadn't stunned it with the frying pan it would've had my throat out.' My mum was babbling. Then she started shouting in rage. 'How the hell did it get into the house? Whose is it, what's it doing here in the first place?' she yelled furiously. 'God,' she added, 'I thought my heart was going to stop. Oh, God!'

'It came up the stairs after me, it tried to get into my room.' Adam was half in tears. Adam's two years younger than me. I'd obviously terrified them, and despite myself I found myself going, Huf huf huf, which was as near as I could get to having a good laugh. I thought, That'll show them!

'What'll they do to it?' asked Adam.

'Put it down, with any luck – it's mad,' said my mum.

I felt my jaw sag open. I was amazed at the way it did that, and I jumped up to the mirror again to have another look at myself, and I looked so funny – a scratty, hairy mongrel with pricked-up ears and its jaw hanging open in horror and surprise. I waggled my eyebrows at myself – you know what? I was hilarious! A dog that could pull faces! I was in such a state, I didn't know whether to laugh or cry. For a moment I stood there pulling faces at myself and killing myself laughing. My mind was just jumping all over the place. One minute I was gibbering with fear and the next I was giggling at the sight of myself in the mirror, or because I'd scared my mum half to death!

I could have spent hours sitting there looking at myself, but I didn't have time. I mean – it could really happen! They really would put me down. That's what they did with stray dogs, wasn't it? No one owned me. I was mad! A mad dog! My mum was going to get the police to put me down and she'd never even know that she'd had her own daughter murdered!

I had to get out. I had to have a plan. I began pacing up and down the floor. I sat down and scratched my ear and had an idea at the same time. It was this – I'd trick them. I shouted out.

14

'Help! Mum, Adam! I'm trapped up here with the dog!' Then I listened closely.

'God, what a weird bark it's got, horrible!' That was Adam.

'It moves all horribly, too, did you notice? Like it's all wrong,' said Mum and Adam went,

'Yuk, yeah, like it's all sort of like, all . . . wrong.'

'It must have some sort of brain disease,' said my mum, and that was so ironic, you know because she was always saying that about me.

'God, Sandra, what's wrong with you? The way you carry on I wonder if you're all right,' she used to say. It was just typical – as soon as I have any problems she thinks I'm bonkers! Now I was a dog and she was still doing it.

I had to get out of there. I ran to the door and tried to open it but my hands still weren't working. Well, what hands? Paws, paws, paws! I told myself. It was amazing, but I was already thinking to myself, You have paws, Sandra Francy, get used to it! Think paws! Think teeth! I knew I had to get used to what was happening or I'd never get out alive. I jumped up and grabbed the door handle with my mouth, and I could hear Adam screeching.

'God, look, it's at the handle!'

They both started screaming then, and Mum yelled, 'Go up and hold the handle up so it can't get out.'

'No way!' screamed Adam. 'It's too mad, I'm not going near it. The germs'll come through the handle.

15

Ahh, look, it's coming!' he howled. I could hear a clatter – Mum dropping the phone – and then they were both screaming as they ran out of the house. They needn't have worried. I could turn the handle but I couldn't pull the door towards me, it just kept banging onto my feet. I ran across the room, jumped up onto the bed and then the window-sill. Thank God! The window was half open. Half open – but on the first floor. It was miles down, but I had no choice. It was that or the vet. I'd scared Mum and Adam out of the house but they'd be on Jane's or Pete and Silvia's phone down the road. When they heard how scared she was, the police would come fast. But – it was such a long way down! I wasn't sure I had the courage, not even to save my life.

As I looked down, next door's cat Pansy strolled along under the wall. I could feel my ears pricking up. I thought, This is too good to miss! I had to whine under my breath to stop myself barking at her. That cat was going to get the surprise of her life.

I jumped right above her. I was coming down feet first right at her like an atomic attack and as I came I was barking furiously. That cat nearly shat itself! She jumped up, all her fur stood up like a cartoon. She was looking right, left, back, front, to and fro – she was whirling round like a firework, but she couldn't work out where the dog was. Dogs come from all directions, but never from above. There was a glorious second when I thought I was going to get her, I was going to grab her in my mouth and taste her blood, but then she looked up and

16

saw me. Wow! She howled like something in a horror film. She *was* in a horror film!

'Dog attack, dog attack, dog in the air!' I barked. Pansy shot off as if she had a sparkler up her fanny. I thought, Huf, huf huf, hurrah!

Then I landed. My springy doggy legs jerked down and up. I was back on my feet in seconds, limping. It hurt – but I'd done it! I'd saved my life and terrorised next door's cat at the same time and I felt great.

Then I heard my mum out on the street, screaming and yelling at the neighbours. I'd wanted that cat so bad, I'd forgotten my life was in danger. Again! I kept forgetting things. The panic gripped me and I took off, me – I took off at the speed of light. I ran right by Mum, nearly knocking her off her feet. I thought, Serve you right, not even knowing who I am. Then I was round the corner and away, even though my joints were aching after the fall. I bombed down the road. A car screeched, I gasped in fear and ran onto the pavement. Then I stopped. Where to go? Round to Annie's! I dashed up the road and stopped again. Forgot – I'm a dog! I went the other way – Wayne's! But shit! I'm a dog, I'm a dog, I'm a dog. I had nowhere to go! Hide, hide, I thought, and I set off again, no idea in my head about who I was or what I was and where I belonged or where to go, except to run and run until my pads bled and my dry tongue beat the ground.

TWO

I ran and ran, but where does a dog go when she has no home? The streets passed like sideshows from an uninvented entertainment. Withington, Didsbury, Northenden – they all came and went, but none of them meant anything to me any more. I knew nothing. The shops were shadows. The window displays had no scent, no sound, no purpose. I was a dog; I didn't even know what things meant.

My feelings were swinging violently from side to side. One minute I was filled with bursts of joy at the way my feet moved, at the wind on my face, the sights and sounds and the flocking of scents around me. You have no idea what your senses are if you've never been an animal. The thrill of the chase! That cat that I'd nearly caught. Oh, yes, there were still pleasures for me in this world. I promised myself one thing – that before I became myself again, I'd catch a cat and tear it to pieces and lap up the blood as it oozed onto the tarmac...

And then, in the next second I was filled with self disgust. Cat's blood – ugh! Disgusting! I was a *girl*! How could I think such thoughts? You see, the change was still working. First my body, then my thoughts – now even my feelings and desires. How long would it be before I became a dog through and through? How long before I even forgot how to think? At moments like these I felt that my heart was breaking inside me as I ran. I told myself that I must never forget who I was. I'm a girl, I told myself. I'm a girl, I'm a girl, I'm a girl. Just remember, Sandra – you're a girl.

At last my pads began to bleed. I could smell the blood before I saw it, and I turned round in amazement to see a line of bloody pawprints following on the pavement behind me. I was exhausted. I'd ended up on the road to Stockport, near the old allotments opposite the new entertainment centre by Parrs Wood School. It was as good as anywhere else. I limped across the road and found a hole in the fence to slip through. It had begun to drizzle hours ago. I hadn't minded the wet but now at last the cold was getting to me and I wanted shelter. I soon found an abandoned shed with the door hanging half off. There was an old donkey jacket someone had left behind in a heap in a corner. I nosed it flat into a bed and curled up with my nose under my tail, breathing in my own comforting scent. I could feel my ears turning this way and that, following the noises that moved about in the twilight, like a radar set on top of my head. If anyone had seen me, they'd have thought I was just a dog lying down for a bit of a doze, but inside, I was breaking up.

It was just *so* typical of my mum not to recognise me. All right, I was a dog, but she was my *mother*. She should've known who I was even if I'd turned into a clod of earth. Just the thought of what she'd done made me twist about and growl and chew anxiously at the donkey jacket. Screaming in terror when I came into the house, when all I wanted was a hug! As if I'd ever hurt any of them! Ringing the police – trying to get me put down! It was unbelievable! I disgusted her so much she wanted me dead. My own mother! No wonder I felt so betrayed. No wonder I'd turned into a stupid, pointless dog.

I shouldn't have been surprised. She never thinks of anyone else but herself and her precious baby Adam. She's always stamping about the house, being busy, never has enough time for me, oh no – but she always finds plenty time for Julie and Adam. I was just the one in the middle. If it was one of them who'd been turned into a dog she'd have known them soon enough. In fact, she didn't just not love me – she didn't even *like* me. She didn't have the same interests or anything. I couldn't talk to her about anything, boys or clothes or anything. She never went out with me to buy clothes or try out make-up, all that girly kind of stuff. To Mum, clothes are just something to keep you warm and as for make-up – I'm surprised she ever even bothered with make-up. She always says it makes her feel naked if she goes out without it. She doesn't let anyone outside the family ever see her without her make-up on, but she still hates it. When we go to stay with people she always comes down first thing in the morning with her powder and lippy on, but that doesn't mean she's interested in it.

'It's a curse, really. Once you've started using it you feel ugly without it,' she once told me, and when Elizabeth Arden stopped making her favourite colour she was in a foul mood for days, because she had to waste her time going to pick another one. I can spend hours in the shops, picking different colours. I could spend a fortune if I had one.

It amazes me sometimes that we're related at all, because even though we look alike we have such different tastes. Whenever I bought some new clothes or tried out some new make-up, she'd just take one look and say, 'Well, you and I have different tastes, don't we?' And that was just if she was in a good mood! If she was in a bad mood she'd curl her lip and make some tart remark.

'I'd have thought you attract enough attention to yourself already,' she used to say. I mean, how about that for a bit of confidence building towards your own daughter?

I bet if I'd been a boy she'd never have gone on to have a third baby. I was just someone who should have been someone else as far as she was concerned. In fact, I think in her heart she wishes she was a man as well. She behaves like one. I think she's got a bit of y-chromosome in there, actually. Julie and me used to tease her about it.

'Mum the man,' we used to say. Julie used to say she was a man with tits. Just my luck – to have two men as parents, one of them disguised as a horrible ugly old bitch. She should never have been allowed to have children in the first place. Look at me, look how I've turned out. What am I? I'm a dog!

Maybe you think I'm just being bitter, but you can't blame me. She just tried to kill me! It would've been different if my dad had been at home. Or Julie. Just my luck she left home a few months ago. If she'd been there she'd have known who I was. We're good friends, me and my sister. We never got on all that well when we were small, but after she grew up she used to step in and help me out when Mum was being useless. Like the time when I had my first period.

Bloody Adam found out about it somehow. At the time I thought Mum had told him. You know – Sandra's feeling a bit funny today because she's having her first period. She always denied it, but in that case, how did he know? Anyway, he was completely obsessed about it, following me about the house asking me all sorts of personal questions.

'How much blood is there?' he wanted to know.

'I don't know, how should I know?' I told him.

'But you must know. It's your body,' he told me.

'Well, I don't know. It all gets soaked up. Anyway, it hasn't finished yet.'

'Well, how much so far? Go on. A tablespoonful? Two tablespoons? A *pint*?'

'Get off!' I yelled.

'He's just curious, there's no need to shout,' said Mum.

'Well, you tell him how much blood you have,' I told her.

'I'm his mother,' she said crisply, but I think she saw my point.

He was still at it when Julie came back from work. He wanted to know everything. I had the cramps really bad and he was leaning over me hissing, 'Go on, tell me. What does it feel like? Where does it hurt?' When Julie came into the sitting room she heard everything.

'What's this shit? You leave her alone!' she yelled. She shoved him out of the way so hard he cracked his shin on the coffee table and howled loudly, so Mum could hear.

'Julie! Stop that, leave him alone!' yelled Mum, but Julie just ignored both of them.

'Is it auntie? Your first time? How is it?'

'It bloody hurts,' I told her.

'Have you had some pills?'

'Mum said it was best not to.'

'Come on, I've got some upstairs.'

I was really made up. Julie hardly ever invited me to her bedroom. We had to squeeze past Adam on the stairs.

Julie pushed him down. 'Give her some space! Get out the way!'

'He's all right, I didn't mind,' I told her.

'He's a brat,' said Julie.

She gave me some paracetamols, and then we sat down on her bed and had a real good girl talk about pads and tampons and how not to leak in bed and all those things you never talk about to anyone but someone like her, a girl, that you're really close to. We both agreed that Mum was totally useless. It hardly affects her at all. She just charges about, same as ever. Even though she's been having periods for the past fifty years or whatever, she still gets cross about having to deal with all the pads and things. She leaves them all over the house for everyone to see.

'She even keeps them on the kitchen window-sill. What for? I mean!' said Julie.

'She probably changes them while she's cooking,' I said, and we both hissed with laughter.

We talked about everything that day. We told one another all these amazing stories we'd never told anyone before, ever. It was a great talk. I thought at the time it was about the best conversation I'd ever had. I thought of poor Adam lurking around the house on his own. He couldn't join in. What did he have to add to a conversation like this? Nothing!

'I bet boys don't have this sort of talk, do they?' I said.

'No way!' said Julie. 'They can't talk about anything. They're too scared to even talk about their dicks in case it turns out they've got a small one.'

'Do many of them have small ones?' I asked her, and she said,

'As far as I'm concerned, *all* of them have small dicks!' and we cackled like a pair of hens.

'They could talk about the first time they came,' I said, but Julie said,

'No way! They'd be too embarrassed. They spend hours and hours wanking in their bedroom and then they're too embarrassed to even mention it to their best friends.'

We killed ourselves laughing. Then we just went through a list of all the people we knew and how their periods affected them – me, her, Mum, school friends, relatives, Mum's sister Evie, who gets the worst PMT you can imagine. But she's very sweet about it afterwards so she always gets forgiven, which isn't really fair.

That talk made me feel better about all sorts of things – about having periods, and about Mum, too, actually, because it made me realise that half the time when I felt she was getting at me, or not caring about me, she was just being herself, really. She used to do it to Julie, too. We sat there and told each other all these stories about all the things Mum had done to piss us off and you know what? We both felt exactly the same. I was amazed. It was so good to know that Julie felt the same way, that it wasn't just my imagination about Mum being insensitive, even if I did get a bit paranoid about her getting at me.

And we talked about Dad. The thing is, although Julie thinks Mum's a bit of a dodo, she feels sorry for her because she thinks she has a hard life. She and Mum get on quite well together but she gets all sniffy about Dad. Me, I think he's all right. He comes over once or twice a year with Eleanor, who he lives with, and we get on really well. We're more alike, but Julie takes after Mum.

She says things like, Well, if he's so great and he loves us so much, what did he go away and leave us for? — which makes me furious. He was leaving Mum, not us.

'Then how come he's not here?' Julie always says, which isn't fair; but it's true in a way as well, even though I don't know what else he could have done.

That's the way our conversations about Dad usually go, but this time she told me this thing which just amazed me. It wasn't amazing in itself. What was amazing was that I'd forgotten all about it. Apparently, see, Dad came in to talk to us the day before he went away, to tell us how much he loved us. I couldn't believe my ears.

'I don't remember that,' I said. All I could remember were the arguments and the shouting and not knowing what was going on.

'You must do,' she said. 'He came in and sat on the bed and woke you up.' I was furious with Julie for not telling me before, but she thought I knew. She thought that all the time I was saying those things about how Dad wasn't leaving us but just Mum, and how he loved us and would really, really love it if we could come and live with him if only it was possible and all that — she thought that all the time I was just repeating what he'd said that night. Because that's exactly what he said — all those things.

'I thought you knew,' she said. 'Whenever we talk about it you repeat what he said almost word for word.'

Word for word! Isn't that amazing? Word for word. So I must remember everything he said and yet I can't remember anything at all about the visit. I tried and tried and racked my brains, but there was just this empty space with nothing in it. Isn't that the strangest thing? Julie said I was sitting on the bed like a little ghost, I was so pale. And then I went to sleep straight away afterwards, while she lay awake for hours.

I think the world is full of wonderful things, mysterious things that no one can ever understand. It was eight years ago, I was nine years old when my Dad left, and that night must be burned into my memory because I repeat what he said almost word for word but I don't remember a thing about it. Isn't it funny how a stupid thing like your period can open up a whole world like that? After that, me and Julie were good friends. We found out how much we have in common, I suppose. Both of us had our dad go away when we didn't want him to.

I woke up whining in the middle of the night thinking about these things. I was sobbing, but the really terrible thing was – and it made me shake and tremble to realise it – that I didn't have any tears to shed any more. I used to have so much when I was a girl – my friends, my family, my home, even school which I'd hated, really. Now I was a dog and I had nothing, not even tears. I only had myself – my four feet, my mouth and my nose.

I pushed my nose back under my tail but sleep wouldn't come. I was wide awake with misery. I stood up and sniffed about and – Oh, that shed was so full! Full of damp cotton and wet wood, cold earth and mould. Outside in the night things were really brewing. Mouse, rat, rabbit, cat — the wind was travelling across the earth bearing so many different people and places to me. The dug earth, the vegetables and other plants pulling goodness out of the ground, the daffodils and the buds, the birds sleeping in the trees, the slugs and snails, the filthy road beyond the fence, the dew on the ground — the night itself had its own scent. I thought to myself, Maybe being a dog isn't so bad. But even the thought that I could enjoy being a dog made me miserable. There was a fox somewhere and I tried a bark, but my heart wasn't in it. My voice echoed off the wooden walls of the old shed and only made me feel how abandoned and lost I truly was.

I lay down again. Memories tumbled around me.

Sometime later I heard someone — something — approaching my shed. A dog — no, dogs! Two of them, stinking of dog pee and the night air, with a fresh kill on their breath. Out hunting for rabbits or rats or some little bitch, but they'd found me instead.

I backed into a corner. I had a human desire to hide but I knew you can't hide from a dog, the slightest atom of you in the air leads him to you. A second later I could hear a breath at the door and smell teeth and spit and stinking meat. I growled, but there was just a sniffing in reply. Were they friendly? What did I care even if they were? It was dogs, wasn't it, and that's something I'd never, never be!

A muzzle showed at the door and one of them came inside. A pair of cold grey eyes looked at me, the eyes of an animal.

'So you're the new bitch,' said the dog, and I broke into a fit of barking.

'We knew he'd done it again,' said another voice from outside the door. 'He stank of guilt. We've been tracking you. Look! You're not alone.'

I could barely make out a word of this, I was barking so frantically. Talking dogs! That was horrible! Dogs that could think – ugh! It made me feel sick. They scared me so badly I actually peed a few drops. I crouched down in shame and rage and terror, my teeth bared, my lips drawn right back over my gums.

'Back off! Back off! Back off!' I barked. But the dog in the doorway just stood watching me. I stopped barking and crouched as low as I could, growling a warning deep in my throat.

'Barktown, California, in the US of A!' sang the dog. He rolled his eyes, lolled his tongue out and wagged his head about so that his tongue thrashed from side to side. Just for a second I thought he was mad – but then I realised: he had a sense of humour. The dog was trying to be funny. But do you think that made me like him any better? No way! Dogs with a sense of humour? Yuk! I began barking at him louder than ever.

Keeping his eye on me the grey dog eased his way backwards out of the door. 'We'll be back,' he growled. There was the sound of feet in the grass and their scent sank. I dashed after them, just as far as the door, still barking madly, and sniffed the ground where he had stood. Hmm – hot treacle, piss, warm grease, burnt cabbage and perfume. How can I describe it? Not bad. Then I stuck my nose outside to get a taste of the other one. He was tawny – burnt porridge, mud and new clothes. I remember thinking, Yes, even colours have a smell. Then I felt sick and had to go and lie down on my donkey jacket.

In the quiet, on my own, I remembered what they'd said: 'You are not alone.' What did that mean? Did dogs have a language all the time and I'd never known? I began to regret seeing them off so fast. I needed company. Maybe they could tell me something about what was happening to me.

I didn't have to wait long to see them again. They were back within ten minutes. I jerked to my feet, but I managed not to shout at them this time. There was another scent with them. It was something nice – something warm and sweet and hot and delicious. I was confused at first. It smelt so good – I thought it might be a spicy chocolate cake getting cooked in the oven, but I knew it couldn't be that. Then the mad dog's head appeared round the door with something grey in his mouth. I couldn't take my eyes off it. He came a little further until he was half in, half out. The other dog stuck its head in the door behind him. He was smaller than the first one, one of those grubby terrier types with springy little legs and greasy fur.

The big dog dropped the rabbit on the floor. 'Peace

offering,' he said. I looked down at the thing – a just-dead rabbit – then back to him. 'Hungry, eh?' he said.

I was – and the rest. I'd had nothing all day apart from a bowl of cereal when I got up and a packet of crisps. That rabbit – I'd never smelt anything so delicious. It had stopped smelling like cake and started smelling like a plate of chips with salt and vinegar on. My senses still hadn't settled down yet.

'Come and get it, baby!' said the dog in a stupid voice. I didn't want to go near him, but the rabbit was irresistible. I eased forward, snatched it in my jaws and sprang away to the furthest part of the shed, where I sank to my belly and began to lick and gnaw at it until the juice ran. I never let my eyes leave those dogs, though. I kept my body raised on my legs, ready to spring up if I had to, and I kept up a low growl in my throat to warn them to keep back.

The smaller dog started sniffing away in the corners and along the walls, exploring the place, but the other dog stood still and watched me. He was one ugly-looking mutt. He was covered with a grimy stubble of grey hair, caked with muck and dirt on his underside, with black eyebrows sticking out of his head like a pair of beetles. His ears started off sticking up, but then bent over and hung down half way up. He had long lean legs and a long lean body, and a muzzle like a rat's with his eyes sticking out too far like round pebbles out of his face. He had a long pink tongue that was hanging out of his mouth, and he stood there with his nostrils flared sucking my scent in and staring at me.

'My rabbit,' I growled.

'Your rabbit,' he agreed. He backed off into a corner and sat down on an old grow-bag with his legs spread and his front half up in the air so he looked like an old man sitting there. Then he lifted one paw to his muzzle and pretended to take a draw on a ciggy.

'Oh, baby, you and me, hmm? We was made to be together, baby, wuz'n we? Cheese an' pigs, baby, parrots and pork, ham an' grass, baby, that's you an' me. Bacon and babies, baby, that's us. What is it, baby, doncha love me any more, baby? Don't you love me? You're not gonna leave me are you, Susanna? NOOOOO!' He put his paws over his head and howled at the roof.

'Shut up, you freak,' I told him, but it was pretty funny actually – that weird-looking dog sitting there like a man, talking gibberish and howling at the ceiling.

'Oh, Christ, Fella,' groaned the sandy dog, but he was laughing at the same time.

The bigger dog sat back up, crossed his legs like a man and twisted his dog lips into a horrible parody of a human grin, which made me growl louder than ever.

'Hey, watch me, I'm a Disney dog!' he said, and he jumped up to his feet and started bouncing round the shed on four legs like Tigger in Winnie the Pooh.

'The wonderful thing about Fella,

'My face is a wonderful farce,

My life is made out of paper,

My tail is attached to my arse,' he yodelled, and I couldn't help it any more, I just cracked up.

'You're mad,' I told him, and straight away he started rushing around the shed spitting and howling,

'Mad dog! Mad dog! I'll bite yer, I'll bite yer! Ooooo, ma rabies is reeeel baaaad today, baby! Arg!' And he fell over sideways and lay on the floor frothing at the mouth. 'TB. Leprosy. The common cold. Everyone has their own poison.'

He was really off his head. He was lying on the ground going, 'Ih, ih, ih, ih,' like he was a machine or something. The other dog was killing himself laughing, and kept glancing at me to see how I liked it. I rolled my eyes and crunched the rabbit's skull between my teeth.

'Just sit still, will you?' I asked him. 'For God's sake.'

The dog got off the floor and walked over to me. He sniffed at my head.

'Thanks for the chips,' I said.

'What?'

'I mean, the rabbit.'

'No prob. I was gonna make a soufflé, sweetheart – candles, the fur arranged tastefully in little balls on the side of the plates, you and me . . . '

'Shut up, please shut up.'

'Right.' The dog sighed, and lay down next to me. After a minute or two the other dog came and lay on the other side of me. I raised my fur and growled slightly.

'OK, OK,' said the smaller one, but didn't move. I didn't say any more. It was kind of nice having warm creatures on either side of me, but I was a bit worried about my rabbit, so I got up and went to lie down in a corner to finish it off. The smaller sandy dog sat up to watch me eat. 'So – what's it like being a dog?'

'You should know.'

'But what's it like for you, baby?' said Fella.

I started to wonder if I should tell them that I was really a person, when I remembered what they'd said earlier about me being the new bitch, and someone feeling guilty. I looked across at them.

'You ... what was that you were saying earlier?' I asked, although I knew the answer already. No dog ever came on like that. 'You're not dogs, either, are you?'

'Oh, I'm a dog, love, I'm a dog all right,' said Fella. 'Y'know, I just can't help it.'

'You're like me!'

'We've all been turned. That's why we came,' said the smaller one.

'How did you know?'

'Your scent. We found your trail by the Mersey at Northenden. We ran back and found Terry. We've been tracking you all night.'

'Oh, yes, you're one sweet-smellin' little bitch,' said Fella.

'Who's Terry?' I asked.

'Terry – the drunk.'

'The drunk? That old alchie? He did this to you, too?'

34

'Oh, yes. You're not the first, and you won't be last, either.'

'You wanna know the story?' said Fella. 'Oh, there's a whole history. Me and Mitch here, we got the whole thing worked out. There's dogs and bitches running around that ain't what they seem. Maybe it ain't just dogs. Maybe the Buddists are right – maybe you've just eaten your own grandmother.' He nodded at the remains of the rabbit between my paws and made me gulp at the thought. 'Maybe,' he went on, rolling onto his back and flipping his paws in the air, 'maybe there's human beings wandering around that ain't what they seem. Well, all you need to know is this: you are one lucky, lucky bitch. You have had the great good fortune to be turned into a dog. Baby! Your life has just begun.' He let his head loll backwards so he was looking at me upside down, and wriggled closer to me. I growled and pulled my rabbit away.

'I don't know what you're talking about,' I growled.

'Mitch, tell her about it. But first, introductions – Oh, yeah, this is the best bit,' barked Fella. He and Mitch jumped to their feet, ran round behind me and stuck their noses under my tail, and without even thinking I got up too, and the three of us walked round and round each other, sniffing away at those . . . special places. It was intoxicating. It wasn't until afterwards that I thought, What's this, I hardly even know these guys and there I was rubbing my nose around their private parts.

'Woof! Better than shaking hands, you bet!' said Fella

35

at last. He flopped down in a heap. Mitch plonked his bum down next to him and had a good old scratch. Outside, there was a noise — a barking, squealing sort of noise, and the ears and eyes of both dogs turned to the door.

'Don't go. Tell me about Terry,' I begged.

Fella rolled onto his back. 'Tell me a story, Mummy. Tuck me up. I wanna glass of water. Blow me a kiss, mwa, mwa, mwa. OK. Mitch. Begin. Our creator.'

Mitch dropped down onto the floor with a crash, laid his chin on Fella's chest and sighed deeply.

'It started when he was about six or seven as far as we can make out,' he began.

'How do you know all this?' I interrupted.

'He talks. Me and Fella have both hung around with him for a while. You may have seen us.'

So that was it — I knew I'd seen one of them, if not both of them before. Terry had been on Copson Street for years, and there was often some poor old mutt tied to his wrist by a piece of string. If only I'd known — those dogs were human beings all the time!

Mitch went on with his story. 'The first person he turned was his own mother. She took some toy or other from him and he threw a tantrum. Next thing is, his mother's a dog.'

Fella chuckled to himself. 'Imagine,' he said. 'Poor kid!'

Mitch rolled his eyes. It was obvious it wasn't Terry who got his sympathy. He went on with the tale. 'Of course, she completely panicked and the tragic thing is, she ran out into the road right under the wheels of a car.'

'Right before his eyes,' said Fella. 'Great start to life. You turn your mother into a dog and she gets killed – bang!'

'Just like that,' I said.

'Just like that.'

'What happened next?' I begged.

'So of course little Terry goes screeching round to a neighbour and explains what's happened.'

'"I turned my mummy into a bitch!"' mimicked Fella.

'The neighbour tries to calm the child down,' went on Mitch. 'She goes round to the house but there's no one there. The child is having hysterics, she can't do anything with him. His father gets a call at work – he was a warehouse manager – and gets told that his wife has gone missing and his son has gone mad.

'And on it goes. The little boy tried to explain what had happened, but what chance did he stand? Who was going to believe him? Obviously something terrible had happened, and the adults came to the conclusion that the trauma was so bad, Terry blamed himself and invented this ridiculous story to explain it away.'

Fella sat up and shook his head. 'Of course, nine times out of ten, they'd be right. People are always doing that sort of thing. Guilt is second nature to a human child. And the grown-ups are even worse. They think they're responsible for everything, even when it's nothing to do with them – even when it's not even any of their business. They can't help it. They're lost without it. Did you know that once a person has children they can never sleep peacefully at night again for the fear of something happening to their brats?'

'That's not true, I had kids, I slept like a log,' said Mitch.

'If you slept, I bet your wife didn't.'

The two dogs started to argue about it, but I interrupted and asked them to get on with the story. Fella lay down again with a sigh and Mitch went on.

'Anyway, you can imagine how it went. Turned his mother into a dog! He mustn't think such things! Of course he hadn't, it was nothing to do with him! The dog who ran into the road and the disappearance of his mother were unconnected. Everyone did their best to convince him that what he knew to be true, was false. When the mother didn't return the police were called in. Then of course it was the shrinks and the doctors, all trying to winkle out out of him what really happened. What chance did the boy have? Pretty soon he came up with a story to satisfy them – he told them a bad man had come to the door and taken his mother away. He said the bad man kept calling his mother a bitch over and over again, which explained the connection about dogs.

'In front of little Terry's horrified eyes a huge, nationwide murder investigation was started up. Interviews with the police on the TV, reconstructions of the imaginary crime, big headlines, public appeals for information, the lot. It went on for weeks. Of course, the murderer was never found, the body never recovered. Terry pretty soon convinced himself that the kidnap story was true – how could all those adults be wrong about something so important? The authorities were very good. He had therapy, counselling, no trouble was spared, no expense. How were they to know they were just making things worse?

'The father was under suspicion for a while, but eventually things settled down. The child's grandmother helped look after Terry while his dad continued his job. He got on with his life, managed to keep things under control. It may be that he did it again during those years. Terry says not, but when you talk to him, there are hints. A schoolfriend, a teacher, a child he met in the playground – who knows? But the next big one for him was when he was nine years old.

'After a few years, his father married again. Terry got on well with his stepmother, everything seemed almost back to normal. Fairly soon, a new baby sister came along, who he says he doted on.

'It was another fit of fury that did it – it always seems to happen when he loses his temper. It was something to do with his little sister, he thinks – some fit of jealousy. It was his dad that got it this time – he was doomed really, right from the start. Every kid gets cross with his dad sooner or later. Whatever, there was some argument about the baby, a tantrum, and then the father suddenly found himself on all fours...'

'Canified!' yodelled Fella. '"I told you, Daddy, I told you, but no one believed me!"' he said, once again

39

mimicking a little boy's voice.

'The father must have understood everything at once,' said Mitch. 'He launched himself in a rage of his own (maybe it runs in the family) straight at his son, bowled him over and in a second had his teeth at his throat.

'Enter the stepmother, hearing the ferocious growls and snarls of the terrified animal. She sees her stepson on his back with a dog at his throat. She runs across the room without a thought for her own safety and kicks the father off the boy. Later, miraculously it seems, they discovered not a scratch on the child. The father, even in his fury, was unable to hurt his own son. The dog was forced across the room surprisingly easily with a broom and locked in the toilet. The boy was screaming inconsolably. You can imagine how desperately the poor stepmother rushed around the house looking for her husband, who had been there only seconds before. If she only knew how close he was! The police were called, the dog was taken away, despite desperate pleas from the distracted child.'

'What happened to the dad?' I asked.

'What do you think? There's only one fate for a savage dog who has no owner. The wretched man was put down.'

I whimpered and let my head sink onto my paws. Fella licked my muzzle sympathetically as Mitch went on.

'And so the whole cycle began all over again. No one could understand what had happened to Terry's dad.

Where had he gone? Everything seemed to be going well – and yet he had disappeared just as his wife had done before him. Terry by this time was old enough to understand that the adults had all been wrong right from the start – his mother *had* been turned into a dog, it *was* him who'd done it, and now he'd done the same thing to his father. He was in possession of a terrible, uncontrollable power. He also understood that no one was going to believe him. He did his best for a long time to keep his story to himself, but his stepmother, distraught though she was, was no fool. She guessed that he was keeping something to himself. Under close questioning, he did tell her the truth.'

'I remember how he looked when he told me that,' put in Fella. 'It was, like, his last hope, you know? He still hoped that someone would believe him and help him make sense of what he'd done.'

'But of course, she couldn't accept it,' said Mitch.

Poor Terry! I thought. He'd more or less killed his own mum and dad and there wasn't even anyone he could confess to!

Mitch scratched behind his ear. 'All he could do was wait for it to happen again. He knew how important it was for him to keep his temper – but he was only nine years old! He did his best, but the result of bottling everything up when he was so upset had exactly the opposite effect. It happened again. One day his step-mother heard screams and howls of despair, went up to the room where her daughter slept and found not a child, but a puppy lying in the cot. That was enough for her. I don't know whether she believed the boy or not, but she'd had enough. She took Terry round to his grandparents and left him there. He never saw her again.

'Shortly after, both grandparents disappeared. We can guess where. Then Terry began a miserable round of children's homes, some good, some bad – but they all had this in common: every new life that he set up, every new relationship that he made was doomed. Foster parent after foster parent disappeared. Again and again he was sent back to various institutions, and gradually his behaviour grew so disturbed and strange that no one wanted him any more. After the homes came the young offender institutions, then the prisons, and now, the street. The only things he can form decent relationships with these days are dogs.'

'And cans of Special Brew,' said Fella scornfully. 'Actually he can't even keep a decent relationship with a dog. He's too guilty about what he's done, poor sod. It's ruined his life. Every time he gets close to someone – bang! They get turned into a dog. Makes a reeeeeeal mess of your social calendar.'

'Poor sod! Poor *us!*' exclaimed Mitch. He seemed to be overwhelmed by his own story and laid down his head with a whine.

In the silence that followed, I turned over what he had just told me in my mind. It was impossible – and yet I knew for myself that it had really taken place.

'Has anyone ever turned back into a person again?' I asked.

I saw Fella glance at Mitch who shrugged. 'We're not sure,' he said, but at the same time Mitch said,

'I think so. If he can do it one way, why not another?'

'Who knows what's possible?' growled Fella. 'Who knows how many little kids there are who can do any sort of miracle? But is that what you really want?' He sat up, and peered intently at me. 'You know what the best thing that ever happened to me was? This. Being a dog. It smells better, it tastes better, it feels better. You don't have your stupid human judgement getting in the way. A dog's days are short, but his moments are pure. Just now you're still in shock, but you wait a few weeks – you'll find out. You think what's happened to you is awful, some sort of disfigurement, some sort of handicap. It's not. It's a miracle. You are more than you have ever been before. You're wonderful and beautiful – no really, every dog is beautiful. Take my advice. Don't worry about being human. You're better off as you are.'

I could hardly believe what I was hearing. 'You *like* being like this?' I asked. Who on earth would rather be an animal than a human being? But Fella nodded.

'You better believe it,' he said. I looked across to Mitch to see what he thought. He caught my glance, looked sideways at Fella, and then shook his head.

'I can't forget my old life,' he said. 'If I could let go of the past, maybe I'd be happy. But I can't. I had a wife, I had two lovely kids. My family was everything to me. A dog can never have those things, not in the same way. It's drop 'em and then move on for a dog. And then, what about my career? What dog ever had a career? I had a good job. I was a teacher, head of department. I had respect!'

But Fella was growling away under his breath.

'See what I mean? He was a teacher, and he still is — still thinking, Could-do-better, must-work-harder, must do this, must do that, all that shit. You don't deserve to be a dog, Mitch, you shoulda stayed trapped as a man, it's wasted on you. You got nothing to worry about any more, and there you are still worrying about it. Stoopid!'

'But I had so much! What torments me is, it's still there, but I can't touch it. Every day I see my wife and my kids. I still love them. And the kids I used to teach going to and from school, my friends, my colleagues at work — they used to turn to me for advice, you know. Now, they're all completely beyond my reach. It was different for you, Fella. You had nothing.'

'I had nothing because I chose nothing, not because I wasn't able to get it,' said Fella, all the time watching me out of the corner of his eye to see whose advice I was going to follow. I could see he wanted me to stay with them. I was flattered. But I'd already made up my mind.

'I could have had the job, the qualifications, you know that,' Fella went on. 'But what for? I never wanted to be a human being anyway. I mean, no one asked me, you know? I wasn't, like, given a choice — it was just dumped on me. And I knew, you know, all along I knew I wasn't cut out for it. There was something wrong. I was like one of those people born in the wrong body, only in my case, it wasn't the wrong sex, it was the wrong species. Trans-species, that's what I am. Being born into a human body was like being born in a prison cell for me. You wake up each morning, you get on with your life, but all the time you have this feeling – is this it? Is this really *it*? This flabby body, this dull nose? Worry worry worry. Work wife kids dead. And that's if you're lucky! I mean, that's what people actually *want* out of life! And if you're not lucky then it's booze drugs dead. I mean, who cares? You know? You know what I mean?'

I nodded carefully. The thing was, I knew *exactly* what he meant – in fact, that could have been me talking! I must have said that sort of thing, or at least thought it, for half my life. On the other hand, I didn't want to agree with him because – you know – because agreeing with him would mean agreeing to be a . . .

'So what's so great about being a dog, anyhow?' I asked.

'What's so great? You ask that? Your nose! Your mouth, your feet under you – the whole goddamn thing! The freedom to be yourself! You know what I mean? If you wanna sniff it, you sniff it. If you wanna lick it, you lick it. The hunt – eh? Imagine that! Hunting with the pack! When you hear the pack in full cry – now, that's living! Sniffing down the edges of the pavement! Bitches on heat! Hot wet blood! Cats! Man, that's living!'

I found I was lifting myself off the ground I was so excited, my legs tense under me, ready to leap forward as if that cat was right there under my nose. Carefully, so no one could see, I lowered myself down. I could see Fella watching me, so I shrugged as if it didn't really matter to me all that much.

'Cats, yeah, it'd be good to catch a cat before I get back to being myself,' I admitted.

Fella smiled as if he could see right through me. 'One day, they'll have the technology to turn people into dogs, just like they have sex change ops today. You'll see people coming out of the closet then, you bet! Yeah! At the moment people just know something's wrong but they don't know what it is. How could they? But when the option is put in front of them – you'll see. There'll be packs of us wandering about then! And it won't just be dogs! It'll be, I dunno, horses! Wolves! Bears! Cats maybe. Now, that'd be some hunt!'

'That's not a hunt, that's murder!' snapped Mitch, who'd been growling away under his breath at this talk. 'You're not a dog, Fella – you're a man in a dog's body. It just happens to suit your lifestyle. You never cared for anyone, you never wanted to be responsible for anything or anyone. That's not a life. That's just existing from day to day.'

'Exactly,' laughed Fella. 'What could be better? Day to day is all anyone ever has. You wanna spend the rest of your life worrying about what happens tomorrow and regretting what happened the day before, fine – but not for me. No way. I'd rather die in a ditch tomorrow than spend one second worrying about it. Living for now — that's what I call life!'

All the time, Fella was watching me, hoping for me to come out on his side, but tempting though it was, I couldn't do it. If I'd known that my wild ways were going to end up like this, I'd have given them up a long time ago. Me, I wanted my life back, no matter how boring and dull and stressful it was going to be.

I got to my feet and went to peer out of the door. The dawn was underway. I could hear cars going past on the nearby road.

I looked over my shoulder at my two new friends. 'I'm going to find Terry. I want to be myself again.'

'Liked school, did you?' sneered Fella.

I shook my head. 'I just want it back. All of it — the good bits and the bad bits. Everything. I know my life wasn't much, but it was all I had. Half my problems were my fault anyhow.'

'Typical human reaction,' scoffed Fella. 'Could have been! Should've been! All my own fault! You really wanna go back to that way of thinking? Listen — there's a whole life out there! Smell it!'

For a second my nostrils flared as I tasted the wealth of life coming in through the open door of the shed, and I was tempted, I admit that — I was tempted. But then I shook my head firmly.

'I miss my friends, I miss school, I miss my mum, I miss everything. I don't know much, but I know this much: I'll never be happy as a dog. That's all.'

Fella rolled his eyes and sighed, but he didn't try to stop me. I thanked them for their advice, and I left them as the dawn was spreading over the houses. I padded silently as a fox along the pavements to Copson Street to try and find Terry, or at least to pick up his scent and begin tracking him down.

THREE

My tireless feet carry me.
I'm a passenger with feet like these.
Who needs cars?
Who needs the wind?
When you have tireless feet
You can double back a thousand times,
you can go anywhere.
Distance doesn't count,
You poor, flat-footed ape.

Terry wasn't on Copson Street that day, but he'd left trails all over from Sainsbury's to half way up the Palatine Road. You couldn't miss it – sweet sweat, beer and pee, same as all drunks; but there was something else to his scent which I can't describe to an animal as nose-blind as a person. It was indescribable. It was the smell of what he could *do*.

The freshest trail led to the refuge on the Palatine Road. The sky was the colour of pale cheese. I lay down to wait but all the people passing by kept watching me and it made me nervous, so I got up and began to walk. I wasn't worried about being back on time to meet him,

I knew I'd catch up with him. When you have a nose like mine, who needs appointments? I'd find him when I wanted to.

As I roamed the streets of Manchester, I thought about the story Mitch told me. It was a terrible thing, but one bit of it kept making me laugh. It was the part when the stepmother had gone to her cot and found not a baby, but a sweet little puppy lying there instead. That brought back fond memories for me, because when I was a little girl, I had a puppy that I loved and I used to do just that very thing with him – lay him in my toy pram and wheel him about like the baby he was. When he still had his big puppy feet and his fat little puppy face, and his round little pink puppy tummy and his little puppy widdler, I used to think that he was the most lovable thing in my whole life.

His name was Ed. My dad gave that puppy to me. He used to chase bits of stick and spoons tied to string round the house like he was a kitten, but to hear him growl you'd think he was a lion instead. I used to put him in the pram and tuck the blankets up around his chin, and put a little bonnet from one of my dolls on his head and put a dummy in his mouth. He lay there for hours and let me wheel him around in the pram. I even tried to breastfeed him from my flat little pimples, but he just licked my face. He let me burp him though. He was so gorgeous. He made me laugh, but I was deadly serious about him as well, and it made me furious when Mum and Dad used to laugh at me playing with him.

Julie used to scold me, she said it was cruel, but Ed liked it. He never put up with anything he didn't like. He could be a very naughty baby, sometimes. I spent ages trying to find ways of putting nappies on him but he always chewed them up. My friend Annie came round with some tiny new-born nappies that she'd got through the post. They were a free sample because her mum had had a new baby the year before and they were always getting things like that. We spent ages trying to get Ed to wear it, and when he did for a little while we were dying to get him to do a widdle.

'I'll change him, it's my nappy,' said Annie, and of course I said that it was my puppy.

'Just because he's your puppy doesn't make it your widdle,' said Annie. I offered to let her change him if he did a poo, but she said no, so I said I'd do the widdle as well, then, so I got her there, didn't I? But then Mum came in and made us stop in case he got the habit round the house. He chewed my Gabby doll's head off one afternoon when he got locked in my bedroom, and I smacked his bottom and put him in the cupboard while he cried and I felt so guilty afterwards I wanted to jump out of the window. I don't know how people ever bring children up, I don't know how they manage to smack and punish them. Even though I know it's necessary, it would break my heart. I'd just feel so guilty.

I thought, Woh! Now I'm a dog maybe I don't have to get guilty about things, if what Fella had said was true. Now, wouldn't that be a gas! That'd make bringing up babies a lot easier.

When he was three years old Ed disappeared, we never found out where. Adam used to tease me by saying that he'd seen him sleeping by the side of the road. I cried my eyes out, but secretly I was relieved because I wasn't interested in him any more. I never liked him so much after he was grown up. I didn't like taking him out for walks. I couldn't be bothered, really. I'd stopped loving him. Isn't it awful, that you can stop loving just like that, just because it's not convenient any more? I know he was only a dog, but still. He used to make me cross by sitting up and staring at me with his clever brown eyes, begging me, just begging me to take him out to the park when I'd just got home from school and I was tired and didn't want to go anywhere. It made me furious, but I knew he was only doing what a dog does, and that I was getting cross because I was so guilty for not looking after him properly.

'I haven't taken him out today and I'm not going to,' my mum would say, and I'd say,

'I don't care,' but I did, but I still wouldn't take him out. It was such a shame because going to the park was the only thing Ed lived for, the only time he really came alive. Sometimes, I used to let him out of the back door on his own, which was an awful thing to do. I used to pretend he'd escaped. Mum and Dad used to threaten to get rid of him if it kept happening. Dad said he'd cause a car crash and people might get hurt and then we'd have to pay.

I never told anyone, but I think I might have let him out that day he disappeared. He could have died on the road and it'd be all my fault.

I had this horrible thought as I was trotting along. It was this: what if Ed had been a person, like me? What if Terry had done the same thing to him? Maybe he knew somehow that the same thing was going to happen to me and that was why he'd come to be my dog. He'd been sent to protect me, but I blew it by letting him out on his own so he got run over!

Then, for no reason at all – and this shows what a truly awful person I am, because it was right in the middle of thinking how I'd betrayed him – I suddenly thought of all the things he'd seen me do. In private. You know? Imagine, if he'd been a person all along. The things he'd seen me do in the privacy of my own room! You know what I mean – having a diddle down there. It made me blush from my nose to my tail! Oh really! I could feel myself going red under my fur. How awful – and he would have been a boy! I used to pretend he was sometimes, when I was small, which is pretty pathetic, but I was only a kid.

And then, you know, I saw the funny side of it and I started laughing to myself. I sat down on the pavement and went, Huf huf huf down my nose, because now I was a dog, I mean – who cares? Dogs come and dogs go. We don't have to worry about things. You can do what you want. I was finding the whole idea of being ashamed at playing with myself a bit funny. Why feel guilty about that? We dogs, we just do what we want to do. We don't have to trouble ourselves about who we do it with or who else is in the room at the time. What for? It's just natural, isn't it? I sat down and gave myself a good licking right there and then, in the middle of the pavement. I didn't care if the whole street was looking, and neither did the street. It was great.

My friend Annie reckoned I cried so much when Ed went away because he reminded me of my dad. She always has those sorts of theories. Ed was my dad's best present to me. When he went away I spent a lot of time comforting myself by cuddling Ed, it's true, but I think Annie is a bit too clever about that sort of thing even though she's good to talk to and always has interesting ideas about your feelings.

Thinking about Ed reminded me of all the things that had gone out of my life – Ed himself, my dad, my boyfriend, who I'd chucked last summer. Now even *I* had gone. It upset me so much I began to howl and groan to myself as I padded along, but pretty soon I noticed how the other dogs and people were watching me. I remembered my mother shouting, 'Mad dog!' and I thought I'd better behave like a normal dog. People are devils, they'll put you down just because they don't know what to do with you.

The day my dad left home was a terrible day for my family, a tragedy that made everything that had gone before it darker as well as everything that followed. Up to then I'd thought our family was safe, but afterwards, I realised that it had been falling down around us all the time. It made me realise that you can never trust anything, because even when things seem to be all right, there can be terrible things happening behind your back, that can affect your whole life, without anyone ever letting you know.

If it was true what Julie said, that my dad came to say goodbye to us and reassure us that he loved us, then that means they must have planned it. And if they planned it, if they had it all worked out, then why was he still there when I got home from school that day he left? Why were they rowing and shouting at each other so that I could hear all the hurtful things they thought of each other? When I have children, the only thing I'll keep hidden from them are the horrible rows and the broken promises and cruel words that people think up to say to someone they used to love.

They were in the hall shouting when I got home that day. Julie must be right, I remember knowing that he was going. I remember Adam was there too – he's like a baby in my memory, although he was seven, just two years younger than I was. He was hanging onto Mum's legs and grizzling. She had her hand on his back, but she was too busy yelling at Dad to take much notice of anything else.

I pushed past Mum and Dad and ran straight up the stairs. I stopped at the top to call Ed to me, and he came up quickly, his tail between his legs, and I bundled him upstairs and into my room. They stopped shouting for a bit. Maybe they were embarrassed to be caught like that. Then Julie came home and started crying, and my mum shouted, 'Now look what you've done!' at my dad, as if everything was his fault, and the whole thing started up again.

Then, guess what? I started feeling left out – left out of a stupid row where a family is broken up. I came out of my room holding Ed by the collar so he couldn't get away from me and came to sit at the bottom of the stairs. So then the whole thing was public, like an audience. My dad even said it.

'I've got an audience to go out on, then.'

And Mum said, 'Give the bastard a round of applause,' and she started clapping.

'Shut up!' shouted Julie.

'Don't talk to my mum like that!' shouted Adam at her.

I said, 'Don't go,' and everything went quiet.

Dad stood there looking at me. It had all gone so still. I remember how my voice sounded so small, but how it changed everything.

Then he looked at the ground and then he said, 'All right, I won't go, not now anyway.'

'Are you mad? Go on, go now, go now, go now!' shouted my mum.

Dad stood there, not knowing what to do, looking at me as if I had the whole thing in my hand.

'Do you want to go through all this again? Just go, you've been going all fucking day, go, go, go!' screamed my mum, and she started holding onto her head and pulling her hair about and rolling her eyes from side to side.

'You'd better go,' I said to Dad, because she was scaring me so much, and so he set his mouth into a straight line.

'Right then, I'll go,' he said, and he picked up his bag and went.

About a year later he moved to America and before anyone knew anything about anything, he had a new job and a new family over there. When the letter came my mum came bursting into the sitting room to announce it to us.

'He had her all the time, it's only been a year, one single year and now he's got it all over again, look, a new wife, a new family, a new bloody everything already. See?' she said, as if that made everything plain – as if none of it was her fault.

But I wish he hadn't gone to America. Now I never see him any more.

Annie thinks I feel guilty about Ed because they made me tell my dad to go. It's a stupid theory, I know perfectly well he was going anyway, but it does make me cringe to think about it – me telling my own dad to leave home! I don't think I'll ever forgive him or Mum for making me do that. To be fair, both of them spent ages trying to heal the wound; they told me over and over it had nothing to do with me, it was going to happen anyway, and so on. But they would, wouldn't they? It just means I can't trust a word they say.

Both Mum and Dad are always saying that I'm more

trouble than the other two put together. That might seem a terrible thing to say, but they're right. See, I'm trouble; I like it. I'm the black sheep, the odd one out. Adam and Julie like bands like Hologram Nights or The Cat Calls or Someone Else, but I just like Acid and House and Garage – the louder the better. I'm like my dad and the others are like Mum. Mum teaches Geography at a high school, but Dad is a business man. He used to own a garage and sold second-hand cars in Oldham. Now he lives in Seattle, USA and sells second-hand Cadillacs to rich Americans. He looks out for himself, but he knows how to live, and how to give. I'd rather be like him than like my mum any day.

'You're just common,' Julie used to say.

'You don't care about anything, do you?' said my mum.

'Why can't you *concentrate*?' my teachers said. 'It should be easy for someone as bright as you if you'd just think about it!'

'You don't do anything you don't want to,' said Adam.

'You don't care about anyone except yourself.'

That was Simon, my old boyfriend, who said that. He loved me. I loved him, but what he never realised is this: love comes easy to people like me. I need a better reason to stick with a boy than just love.

It's right that I don't think. I just do. I don't like thinking, or reading. Now that I'm a dog I expect I'll forget how to read altogether and you know what? I don't care. As for feelings – well, they're things that just happen, aren't they? I want to have a good time. I had friends like Annie with all her psychology, and she's great, you know, she's my best friend, or she used to be, anyway. But the people I feel most alive with are people like Wayne, Dobby and Michelle – people you can know and then forget about all in a week. The sort of kids my mum wouldn't let in the house, who just want to run out on the streets kicking cans and getting touched up and sticking chewing gum onto old ladies' hair while we're queuing in a shop. I did that once. I did it to another old dear with smoke. I was standing behind her with a mouthful of fag smoke and I bent till my mouth was on her curls and I breathed slowly out so the smoke oozed out of her hair like her brains were cooking. We all ran out of the shop yelping like – well, like dogs, really.

As I padded along up the Wilmslow Road, I started thinking again about the alchie, Terry, and I began to see that really, we had a lot in common. We'd both lost our dads – and at about the same age, too. We both felt guilty about what had happened. We didn't fit. I could understand his rage and how lonely he must feel. If my rage had the ability to turn people into animals, half of Manchester would be on four legs by now. Actually, I think he was very restrained only to do it every now and then. I could think of a thousand people I'd like to turn into dogs. I'd have got angry on purpose with them if I could do what he did.

By this time I was getting hungry again. First thing, I turned my paws in the direction of home to go and get a sandwich or something, then I thought – that's out! Then I stood on three legs and started patting my sides. If you'd seen me you'd think I was going crazy, but all I was doing was trying to pat my pockets to see if I had any money in them to buy myself a chocolate bar or something. Bonkers! I still wasn't used to being a dog yet.

I sat down in the road and all these thoughts went through my head, like gravel pouring out of the back of a lorry – go home and get a sandwich, go into a shop and buy something, go round to a friend's and beg something, go to the school canteen and get a lunch – bang bang bang! All utterly impossible! I didn't believe it at first, that those ordinary things should suddenly have become impossible, and the same thoughts came back. I had to go through them all four or five times before it really dawned on me that all the usual ways I had of getting food had stopped dead, just like that. People were tripping over me in the street, so I got up and went to sit by the wall. I felt like crying. I was useless as a person, and now I made a useless dog, too. Only a baby can't feed itself. Even if I had money, who'd sell anything to a dog? Once I'd found Terry – if only he'd agree to be my master! – he'd feed me until I was myself again. But in the meantime, what was I going to do?

I thought of that rabbit Fella had given me, but I was miles away from the allotments. Withington isn't exactly full of rabbits.

Then I had this great idea – a cat! Get a cat! Yeah!

There's not many rabbits on the streets, but there's plenty of cats. All you can smell in town sometimes is cats. Of course, I know what you're thinking – whoever saw a dog catch a cat? They bark at them and they chase them but they never catch them. Cats're just too quick. But I was different – I was a dog with brains. I was certain I could catch a cat, if only I had the right plan.

I started to nose about and found a fresh trail soon enough – the ground was almost warm. I followed it up as quietly as I could. I remembered how cats always slide along the ground when they're hunting and I started to do the same, which made me chortle to myself – a dog hunting cats like a cat! But it was exactly that sort of thing that was going to give me the edge. I found him soon enough, sitting on a garden wall just ahead of me. I crept along, dashed in through the open gate and managed to hide myself behind some bushes next to the front door.

That cat had it coming. I made my plan in the fraction of a second it took me to get in through the gate and into the bushes. I was going to call him to me. It should be easy. Pursing my lips tightly as if I was eating a lemon, and using my tongue half as lips and half as tongue, I was certain that I could still perform human speech – well enough to fool a cat, anyway.

The cat was sitting on the wall, innocent and plump. I made a few practice whispers and then...

'Puss, puss, puss, puss, puss. Here, puss,' I called. Well, it was pretty good. I thought so anyway, but puss was not impressed. He yelped and leapt to his feet, back arched, fur on end. His head turned slowly round to stare at the bushes where I was hidden as if he hardly dared imagine what was hiding there. I kept as still as if I was turned to stone — which wasn't easy. Every fibre in my body wanted to give chase, but I knew if I did that he'd be gone in a blink.

'Here, puss, here, want some fish? Have some milk, pussy-pussy,' I called. Hidden in that bush I made the most outrageous promises to that cat, but the stupid thing didn't know whether to believe or not. He began to back off, still swelling up like a furry balloon, hissing and spitting. And at that moment the door opened and a woman came out.

It was pure chance, but my heart leapt in hope because she had a tin of cat food in her hand. The cat was obviously hers and she wanted it inside. Now she'd do the calling for me! I was right next to her. All I had to do was keep still and let her bring the cat to me. But keeping quiet! Oh, it was so hard!

'What is it, Smokey? What's the matter? Come on, puss! Oh, dear!' she said, because the cat was behaving as if it had seen Satan himself. 'Come on, Smokey, dinner time,' she said. And suddenly it was all just too much. I couldn't contain myself.

'Yes, yes, come and get it, Smokey, dinner time, dinner time!' I roared. The words leapt out of my lips; I sounded like something from hell. The woman screamed, jumped back and slammed the door; the cat yowled and lit off like a firework. There was no point in hiding any more, and I burst out of the bush and jumped for him. The little shit was up the pipe and on to the conservatory roof next door before I could draw breath. As I stood underneath barking at him the tin of cat food came whizzing out of the window and struck me on the shoulder. Looking back, I saw the woman shouting shoo at me. Her face was as pale as milk.

'Thanks!' I barked. I have no idea whether she understood me or not. I grabbed the tin of food in my mouth and limped off down the road into Withington. I had a sore face from where my mother had hit me with the frying pan, and now I had a bruised shoulder as well from the tin. But I had food. When I was far enough away, I dropped it and spent ten minutes pushing it up and down the road with my nose, trying to get at it. Fortunately, the tin was opened, but it was hard work with no spoon and no hands to hold it even if I had one. I tried holding a stick in my mouth and digging it out, but it was slow work. In the end, I had to leave half of it still inside. That little snack had just made me hungrier than ever. What a pathetic creature I was! I needed comfort and food. I *had* to find Terry. I needed a master as soon as possible.

FOUR

By the time I got to Copson Street I was miserable. My shoulder was bruised where the cat food tin got me, my eye was throbbing, my pads were bleeding and I was starving hungry. I picked up Terry's trail at the refuge and followed it past Withington along the Wilmslow Road into town. He hadn't gone far. I found him sitting on a bench next to Sainsbury's with a can of Special Brew in his hand and his coat pulled up to his ears against the early morning chill. There was an old bloke sitting next to him with his elbow on his knee, holding tight to a can of his own.

I was scared. I sat down a little way off where I could get a look. What power this man had! If he could control it, he could rule the world. I sat there and stared through the legs of the commuters going for the bus, and the pedestrians on the street, and I had a vision of a war where Terry was General. What a battle! Squads of soldiers suddenly turning into dogs! Their shouts would become barks and they'd fall forward onto their four feet. The packs on their backs would squash them and they'd have to wriggle out from underneath, and stand around whining and looking surprised. Some of them would try to grab their guns and grenades with their teeth or their paws. A dog trying to fire a gun! There'd be dogs barking inside the tanks, trapped; planes coming down from the sky with a yelping poodle at the controls, trying to seize the joystick in its teeth. Boats spinning aimlessly in circles, machines falling silent! What a weapon! Forget atom bombs, forget bacteriological warfare! Dog them all!

What if he did it to the whole human race? What a paradise the world would be then! No one to open a tin or drive the car or put one brick on top of another. No one to open the window, or lock the door. No one to count the money, or spend it. The pack would come back to the fields and woods and run along the crumbling streets. In my imagination I could see the shops of Copson Street growing dirty and caving in, the pavements sinking, the road breaking up, the grass and trees coming back. Rabbits grazing the car parks! Calves and lambs up for the hunting!

I thought of the city farm down at Wythenshaw Park and reminded myself to pay it a visit.

Then I shook my head and the world of man came back to my eye – stinking cars and food in jars, and the world wrapped up like a toy for big pale monkeys. Sod them!

And there was Terry.

'Master,' I thought. When I was a girl I would have spat on that word, but now that I was a bitch I felt a bubble of love in my heart. What that word meant!

Food, companionship, love. I was sure I could love him. Could he love me?

I came forward slowly, with my head hunched down, my eyes steady on his face, my tail slowly wagging. The old man next to him spotted me first.

'Is that dog yours?' he asked.

Terry's eyes turned and fell on me, and he started. 'God no, nothing to do with me,' he croaked.

The older man glanced at him and raised his eyebrows curiously. 'It seems to know you, that's all. Here, boy...' He put out a hand encouragingly towards me. 'Come on, boy. What's your name, then? Good dog!'

People always assume a dog's a boy, but I didn't care. I let him ruffle the fur on my head and pat my back, but I kept my eyes on Terry. I could smell the fear creeping over him, springing out of his pores. He was inching himself away from me along the bench, his can held hidden under his coat, his legs wrapped round each other tightly. He watched nervously as the other man stroked me, but he didn't offer me his hand.

'Are you all right?' he asked me.

I nodded. The older man laughed and said, 'What a way to speak to a dog!'

Terry grinned weakly. 'Good...girl?' he said, in a questioning tone of voice. He bobbed his head to look underneath me and check, and despite myself, I felt myself blush. He put his hand out carefully, ready to snatch it away if I went for him, but I bowed my head and let him pat me and fondle my ears. Then I licked his hand to show submission. Terry began to smile. I whined and put my paw on the bench beside him.

'She seems very fond for a dog that's nothing to do with you,' said the older man, sounding slightly hurt that I had gone for Terry and not him.

'Oh, I have a way with them, don't I, girl?' smiled Terry. Now that he knew I was friendly his mood had completely changed. He was smiling and squeezing his hands together as if he'd just found a pile of money. He stood up suddenly. 'Here, I've got things to do,' he said.

'Things to do, have you? Oh, well, fancy that,' said the man. 'Something on the Stock Exchange, is it?'

Terry nodded absently and took a few steps away. I followed at his heel. We walked up the road and round the corner and as soon as we were out of sight, he took hold of the loose skin behind my head and shook my head gently.

'I didn't mean to do it, you know. Oh, but you make a lovely dog, you know that? You make a better dog than you did a girl, and that's saying something. I used to notice you all the time, walking up and down the street with your friends. Oh, you were gorgeous, weren't you? And you're gorgeous now. Yes, you are!' He paused and stared at me as if he wasn't sure. Then he got down on his haunches in front of me and held my face in his hands.

'Is it you? Is it really you? Give me your left paw if you understand me.'

I put my left paw up to him.

'Now your right.'

I gave him my right paw.

'I knew it was you! Can you talk at all?'

I tried to say, 'I'm practising,' but it came out sounding nothing like it. Terry laughed.

'Are you hungry?'

'Yeah!'

'What? I can't make out a word. Use your head.'

I nodded. Tears sprang into Terry's eyes and he began patting me and stroking me.

'Oh, you're gorgeous. You are, aren't you? Yes you are. Yes you are! Aren't you lovely, aren't you gorgeous? Oh, I love you, I love you, I love you, you good dog, you good girl, you good good good girl!'

After a time he sighed, stood up and led me up the road to buy me meat. I'll say this for Terry, he took care of me. If I went hungry, he went hungry first. Only the drinking came before I did, but the drinking came before everything, even himself. Oh, I was jealous of the drink.

On that first day we were both so happy just to be together. We walked back into Withington for the butcher and he bought me some dog meat and begged a marrow bone for me – delicious! Then he got some bread rolls from Somerfield's and I wolfed those down too, while he stood and watched, rubbing his can between his hands and laughing at me. It made people look fondly at him – the poor man feeding his dog good food while he stuck to his beer. One woman stopped and gave him a pound.

'See you spend it on yourself this time,' she told him.

'Thank you, ma'am,' said Terry politely. 'That means I can have another drink,' he told me when she'd gone. I pushed a roll towards him with my nose, but he waved his can in the air. 'This'll do me for now, I can't take breakfast so early,' he told me. He leaned forward to stroke me. 'It's the least I can do, you poor girl. God, but I'd change places with you if I could!'

After he bought himself another drink, Terry went round to the café to beg some water. The owner gave him an old plastic bowl for me to drink from, and poor Terry was so delighted and made such a fuss of saying thank you, that he made the man blush with pleasure.

'If that's all it took to make the rest of us happy, the world would be an easy place,' he said.

'Yes, but not for long,' said a woman standing in the dark kitchen behind him. I stood there sniffing – bacon, grease, fried eggs, baked beans, armpits, the perfume from the woman, frying oil – my God! There were times in that first week when the smells of this world threatened to overcome me, like an invasion of my nose.

After I'd drunk my water we settled ourselves down on the pavement. Terry had an old blanket which we shared half each, just as we shared everything. He folded my half over my head and tucked it up under my chin – I must have looked like someone's granny – and gave me a big kiss on the nose, which tickled me and made me huf and lick his face.

'We'll get you a blanket of your own, soon. Maybe

the charity shop will help us out,' he said. He put the drinking bowl in front of us and then took a creased, dirty piece of paper out of his pocket. It read, 'Please help,' in blue biro. He found a pen in his coat and added, 'Dog and self to feed,' underneath. Then he settled himself back.

'A dog is a responsibility,' he told me. 'You need feeding and watering. We should get some jabs for you. There's all these diseases around that dogs get, you know. There's charities for that. There's as many charities for dogs as there are for people.' He ruffled my ears. 'A dog – it's a lot of work. But what can I do? You used to be such a pretty girl, and now you're a pretty dog. Well, girl – you look after me and I'll look after you, eh? That's the way, eh? And I'll call you Lady. OK?'

I said, 'That's the only way I'd ever get to be a lady, then,' and he laughed, although I don't think he understood. He made me so happy, talking to me like that, but already I was losing track of what he said, it was just grunts and mumbles to me. Soon, I slipped away into a lovely, warm doggy doze.

We did all right, me and Terry that day, as far as the money went. All day it was chinkitty-chinking down into my dog bowl. Terry got more beers and got happy, and that made me happy. He promised to love me and I promised to love him. He wept tears and me, poor bitch, I had no tears any more, so I licked his off his face and I whined and held up my paw and rolled over so he could tickle my tummy.

'You forgive me?' he whispered, and I was so grateful that he wanted me to forgive him that I did – forgave him in a second for stealing my whole life off me. The people going past were so touched at the sight of us cooing over each other, the money came down faster than ever – too fast, really. Poor Terry wasn't used to so much money and drank too much beer. By the time the afternoon was half way through he was too drunk to speak, and just about managed to stagger away and find a place out of sight to pass out in, behind a cheap hotel on the Palatine Road. He slept there for a couple of hours – me on guard, and I was proud as a soldier. I was quite prepared to savage anyone who came too near.

Looking back, it's something I can't understand, why I was so grateful to Terry of all people for the smallest little kindnesses he gave me. But I wasn't the first to fall head over heels in love with someone who has destroyed their whole life. The thing is, he was all I had in the world, my last living link to being human. Every little thing I did for him, it felt like he was doing me a favour.

As the dark came, he woke up.

'Jesus,' he said, staring at me in the half light. I perked my ears as prettily as I could and wagged my tail. 'Still want to celebrate, do you,' he said thickly. But it was only more of the same – bread rolls and a slice of belly pork and water for me and a four pack of Special Brew for him. I wanted to walk and play and hunt – I don't know what I wanted! To fetch sticks, anything! – but Terry had finished his day already. He just wanted to get out of it as fast as he could. He took me and the beer back to his shelter – a piece of corrugated plastic behind the hotel – drank the beers one after the other, bang bang bang bang, with hardly a word spoken. Then he staggered off to empty his bladder nearby, rolled himself up in the blanket, pulled a corner of it out for me to lie on, and went straight back to sleep for the night.

I thought, Is that it? A day in the life of a drunk? But I'd made a start. Maybe if he cared for me enough, he could turn me back into myself. What else was there to hope for? I prowled up and down the garden, but I wouldn't go far away from him. I had to protect him. If anything happened to my Terry I'd be stuck like this forever. At last, boredom turned into exhaustion, and I curled up with my back to him and tried to sleep.

But my head was buzzing. It was going to be a long night. I'd been busy all day, but now that I had some time on my hands, thoughts and memories of everything I'd lost came flooding back to me. My family – how was my disappearance affecting them? Did they think I'd been murdered or raped? Most likely they'd think I'd run away from home. That would be just typical of me – to let them run around looking after me and loving me for years and years and then dump them as soon as things got a bit difficult. I'd thought about running away from home so often in the past year – and I'd told them I wanted to do it, too. Only a week or so ago, I'd had a row with Mum and told her that the only reason I carried on living with her was because there was nowhere else to go. She'd shouted and wept, but I didn't care.

My poor mum! Now that the shock of her not recognising me had worn off, I began to see things a little more from her point of view. How could she have known who I was? I barely recognised myself. I was a dog – I was impossible! I was always asking the impossible of people. And now I might never get to tell her how much I loved her and appreciated her.

And it wasn't just my mum either. My dad – had he been told that I'd disappeared? And poor Julie and Adam – what did it feel like for them to have a sister like me, who just used people all the time? I hadn't realised that my life was so full of people who cared for me before that night. My friends at school. Annie, who I'd turned my back on, because she wasn't enough fun. Simon, my old boyfriend, who I dumped because he was too steady and faithful . . .

'Are you sure it's not because you think you're not good enough for him?' That's what Annie said, and I'd laughed at her at the time, but now look – I was a dog, not good enough for anyone any more. All those people gone forever out of my life, and I was doomed to walk the same streets as them and see the same sights, and yet they'd never know me. They'd see me but they'd never know me. If only I could be given back my human voice just for an hour, so that I could tell them who I was!

And it was all my fault. All I'd been bothered about was having a good time. I didn't want any responsibilities or commitments, not even to my own friends. I made everyone unhappy, and I didn't even care.

The funny thing is, it's almost like I *decided* to go off the rails in my life. I can pretty nearly remember the first time it occurred to me that there had to be more to life than what I was getting. It was in my bedroom with Annie. We often used to do our homework together, we'd go round to each other's houses and just work. I was never as clever as her – she was always top of everything – but I never had any trouble with schoolwork, so long as I could be bothered to do it.

It was fun doing homework with Annie because she was a good laugh as well as hardworking. We were doing nets that day, and she was cracking me up by going on about doing a net of her boyfriend's willy and seeing if our teacher could work it out and put it back together again.

'I bet she'd take it home and make it up out of cardboard or something,' she said.

And I said, 'Then she'd bring it in the next day and it would be *ruined*!' And we'd both fall around laughing like a pair of drains.

But all the time we were sitting there laughing, I was thinking, It's all right making jokes and things, but actually, really – I'd rather be doing something else. I'd been thinking like that about a lot of things. About people. My dad, and how he was always on at me to come and visit him in the USA – I mean, why couldn't he come and visit me? And my mum, who I wasn't getting on with, and what a pain Adam was, and how I was bored with school, bored with Annie, bored with Simon. Everyone wanted something off me, you know? Annie wanted me to spend more time doing homework, because our mock GCSEs were coming up. Simon wanted more time with me. Mum said I was going out too much. See? The exact same people who were supposed to be my friends, and all they wanted was me to be someone else. It was just too much.

Annie started on about not going to Planet K that Friday. She thought we ought to stay in and work instead, because of the exams coming up.

'We can't just work all the time,' I said. 'You know how much I like Planet's.'

'Well, I'm staying in. You could go with Simon,' she said, but she knew very well that Simon wasn't going to come. He was working on Friday nights. He was worse than her, he didn't even like me going to a club without him because he was scared I'd get off with other boys. I had to stay in because he was too busy for me! It was stupid. I just wanted to go out and have a good time.

I don't know why, but that just started me off.

'Do you know what?' I said to Annie. 'I don't care. I'm just realising it now.'

'What do you mean? What don't you care about?'

'Anything. This. Work. Getting good results.'

'You need good results, though.'

'One day maybe. But why now?'

Annie just shrugged. 'That's what you do at our age,' she said.

'I can do them later. Or not. But I don't care. I don't care about any of it, really. I just do it, but I don't care really. It doesn't mean anything to me, really.'

She looked at me and laughed. 'You're crazy, Sand,' she told me.

'Yeah, but I don't care. Do you see what I mean? Actually, I don't care about anything. Not even Simon, you know?'

'I thought you loved him.'

'I do, but I don't care!' It made me laugh. I didn't even know what I was talking about, but I knew it was true. 'I could stop seeing him and it'd break me up but I wouldn't *care*. I mean, so what? He's always on at me about things too. I'd miss him, but it wouldn't make me unhappy. I think I might even be more happy. Isn't that weird?'

'And what about me – don't you care about me, either?' she asked, and I said at once,

'Oh, no, I care about you, of course, you're my best friend.' And I went over to give her a hug but, really, she was right. I didn't care about her either even though she was my best friend. Does any of that make sense? All the time I was reassuring her I was thinking, actually, sitting here doing homework with her wasn't my idea of a good time either.

That Friday I went to Planet K on my own, despite Annie and despite Simon and you know what? I thought going on my own was going to be boring and lousy, but it wasn't. It was brilliant. It was just brilliant. I remember

76

coming home about two in the morning, and I knew Mum was going to kill me for being late and not ringing, and I just couldn't care less. I'd met up with this gang, they were great. I was pissed out of my head and I'd had some puff, and I'd walked half the way home with this lad. We didn't do anything, not much anyway, just felt each other up — and it was just brilliant.

'That was just so brilliant. That was just so *brilliant*!' I shouted. I was walking home on my own shouting my face off. 'What am I doing with my life? Why aren't I just doing this all the time?' I yelled.

And after that I couldn't stop myself. I just decided to get off on anything I could find to get off on. I stopped seeing Simon, even though I loved him; I stopped seeing Annie, even though she was my best friend. I stopped working hard at school, even though I wanted a good job. And it was just great. I was *so* much happier. You might not believe it. But I was.

Then of course the shit hit the fan. Everyone was furious. Mum thought I'd gone mad. She got on to Dad so he could ring me up and go on some more at me. On and on and on and on and on, like I was some sort of mad bitch, as if I'd gone crazy. Mum acted as if it was me who had gone all aggressive, but actually it was her. I was as happy as I ever had been, or I would have been if people had let me. She was the one who was going mad. Basically, she was pissed off because I wasn't living the life she wanted me to live. I'd stopped living her life; I was living *my* life, the life I wanted. And you know what? That's the one thing you're never allowed to do. I found that out dead quick.

We had rows about everything. She started having nice cosy long conversations with my dad on the phone. I mean — they'd spent the past seven or eight years barely able to speak to one another and then they start getting on together in order to give me a hard time. What's that all about? They went on and on and on, about my GCSEs, about my boyfriends, about staying out late without telling Mum where I was. Well, there was no point telling her. She said it was to stop her worrying, but that wasn't true. I tried ringing her a few times just to keep her happy, but it never stopped the rows. She just yelled at me anyway.

You should have seen it when my GCSE results came through the door last summer.

'Oh, Sandra,' she said. 'Look at it! And we hoped you were going to do so well! A C in English. English used to be your best subject.'

'It still is,' I pointed out, and she said,

'Yes, but all the others are Ds!' which made me laugh like a drain, although I didn't feel like it. I admit it, I was disappointed, but I still didn't care! I'd made up my mind months before that I wasn't going to put myself out over GCSEs. I was too busy having a good time!

And why shouldn't I? What's so great about school? So you've got to get a job, have you? Well, look at those teachers. How happy are they with their precious jobs? They're all stressed out of their minds. You talk to them

– they don't like it. They spend their whole lives teaching you to go and do what they've done and they hate every second of it. I remember Mr Wales, our maths teacher, when this kid said he wanted to be a teacher.

'I can't recommend it,' he told him. 'The job's not like it used to be. It's a huge amount of work, the rules keep changing. The money isn't as good as it used to be when I started out. Most people find it exhausting. Honestly, I couldn't recommend it any more.'

And that's teaching, which is a doddle. So what does he think the rest of the world's like? I bet it's the same everywhere. My dad used to moan about work. So does everyone else. The hours get longer, you get bossed around, you've got to do as you're told from one end of your life to the other. Well, maybe that's your idea of a life, but it's not mine. I thought, Plenty of time for that when I have to. But right now I'm gonna have fun while I still can!

'All those boys,' my mum said, and she looked at me as if I was the Great Slut of Withington. For God's sake – there weren't that many of them. Eight or nine. Ten, if you count Soppy, which I don't. I was too drunk.

Annie told me that I was going off the rails because I came from a broken home. 'All those boys,' she sniffed. Can you believe she said that to me? Just the same thing as my bloody mum. All those boys. The thing that really annoyed me was, it wasn't allowed for me to *like* doing it. It wasn't allowed for me to have decided I *wanted* to stay out late and try out a few drugs and sleep with a few

79

boys. It had to be because I was upset, or going crazy or something. People like Annie think that people only do bad things because they've got problems, but who wants to be good anyway? Dad left years ago, for God's sake. I was only nine. I hadn't even started High School. It wasn't anything to do with that. I just suddenly started thinking, Here I am, young and beautiful – well, pretty, anyhow – and all I do is stay in and work and worry about things when I should be out doing them. That's how I am. I just want a good time. I mean, OK, I'm seventeen and I've slept with a few boys. Who cares?

People think less of a girl if she sleeps around a bit, and of course I don't want people to think of me as a slut, or a bit of a bike. But I'll tell you this – I'm glad I did it. I'm happy I did it. I don't regret one second – even the bits that were horrible.

I had a horrible argument with Annie the day she said that. She made me really cross with that snotty 'All those boys'.

All those boys, neh neh neh. I said, 'I happen to like it.'

'So do I,' she said, 'but I don't have to go around doing it with anyone who asks. If you find someone you like, that's enough for me.'

And I said, 'What, with Little-Willie? What do you know, if that's your idea of sex?'

'Don't call him that,' she snapped. It was really wrong of me, actually. She'd told me not so long ago that she thought that her boyfriend had a little willy, but she didn't know if it was true, and she wanted me to tell her because I'd seen more than she had. We nearly wet ourselves laughing, trying to work out how big it was. I mean, what do you do? You can't whip out a ruler at the vital time and say, 'Just checking.' I asked her how much of it stuck out above her hand if she held it and she blushed like a little mouse. It was so funny. I teased her when she showed me.

'Is that all?' I asked, and we laughed and laughed at the time. But still, that was then, and me calling him Little-Willie this time really drove her mad. She shouldn't have said that sniffy thing about All Those Boys.

'Little-Willie, Little-Wille,' I hissed, and that was it, we fell out and we've not been friends since. I miss her, Annie, although she was a sniffy cow who always thought she knew best.

Looking back, I can't think of one single person who was on my side. Even Julie thought I was a big blob of scum, same as the rest of them. It happened with her at Swingler's. It was about two in the morning. I was right out of it, dancing and drinking, and loving every second of it and feeling that I could go on for ever. Then Julie turned up with her bloke Angelo. I always called him Angela as a joke – he didn't mind. I hadn't seen her for ages, she moved out to her own flat in Hulme a few months ago and I don't see her half so often any more. We flung our arms round each other and hugged and danced around and screeched, it was great to start with. But then she dragged me off to have a talk.

I hate Julie when she starts on her auntie thing. I

could see it all coming, I could have written the script for her, I'd heard it all so many times. She began by going on about how worried Mum was about me, and that got me off on the wrong foot for a start. Whose side was she on? We were supposed to be friends!

'Friends can worry about you. That's what they do if they're good friends,' she bawled over the music. Which was true of course, but that wasn't the sort of friends I was interested in at the time. 'You just seem to be all over the place at the moment,' she yelled.

'I'm having a good time,' I bawled back. 'I'm *enjoying* myself, that's all.'

'What happened to Simon, then? I thought you were getting on really well,' she bellowed.

'We were,' I howled back. 'We were, that's just the problem.'

'What?'

'That's just the problem. We were getting on *too* well. It was getting comfortable. Look, I'm only seventeen. I don't want to get bloody married, you know what I mean?' It was a real pain, explaining all this at about six thousand decibels. Julie grinned and nodded like she understood what I was talking about, but her words were different.

'You be careful.'

'I am careful!'

She just pulled a face and turned away to swig her drink. Angela came up, and I was hoping she'd finished, but then he left again and she went straight back to it.

'Mum's worried you might be on drugs,' she yelled.
Straight on to the next nag, see?

'Who says?'

'You're on drugs now, I can tell,' she shouted.

'So's everyone else.'

'I'm not.'

'I bet you're about the only one,' I said. That's the
only thing about Julie. She's so prim!

'You don't need that sort of shit to enjoy yourself.'

'No, but it helps,' I told her. She was really getting
on my tits. 'Don't worry about me,' I told her. 'I'm
doing fine, you worry about yourself.'

'Aren't you worried about your GCSEs? You don't
want to blow your re-sits.'

'There's plenty of time for them later on. You worry
about yourself,' I told her, and she rolled her eyes and
said that we weren't talking about her, we were talking
about me. 'No,' I said. 'No, *you're* talking about me.'

'What about these boys, then?'

I said, 'Which one?' and she grinned again, as if we
were being wicked, but it wasn't like that.

'You need to slow down, Sandra. You're gonna catch
something. You're gonna get pregnant.'

'I'm not stupid. I'm looking after myself. I'm taking
care. Stop treating me like a kid.'

'I'm not treating you like a kid.'

'Then stop telling me what to do!'

'I'm allowed to worry about you, aren't I? You're my
sister.'

83

'Just because I'm enjoying myself everyone wants to be my mum.'

'You're only seventeen,' she yelled at me – as if nineteen was the height of maturity. And then it turned into a real row, a real whopper. We both got furious with one another. It went on for ages, us there in all that noise shouting our heads off. Maybe it was because we didn't want it to happen and – you know how it is – you keep expecting the other person to see sense. If only they'd *listen*, if only they'd see it your way! Then I suddenly got sick of it. What had any of it to do with her? I didn't nag her about things. I thought, I'll shag about if I want to. And you know what I did? I swung round and grabbed hold of this bloke who was going past. I'd seen him about with his mates earlier. He was all right, but I didn't particularly fancy him, it was just because he was on his own. I grabbed hold of him and I said,

'Snog me.' He did, right there in front of Julie. She couldn't do anything except stand and stare. When he came up for air I said,

'Get your coat, you're pulled.' And he said,

'What, are you up for it, then?' And I said yes. Just like that. Just to get at Julie. And you know what? Me and this bloke, we went to get our coats and I went back with him and I did it. I actually went through with it, I went home with him and slept with him, just like that. And you know what? It was the horriblest thing I ever did. I didn't even like him, I found that out on the

84

way to his place in the taxi. He lived in this horrible smelly room in a shared house. He must have thought it was Christmas, getting someone like me to go home with someone like him. His breath smelt, he was stupid and rough. I felt dirty and used and horrible even though I'd done it myself. Horrible! I was furious with Julie because she was the one who'd made me do it, she was the one who'd nagged me when I was off my head, and if she hadn't done that I wouldn't have gone and shagged the first bloke who came along.

God, when I look back, I was so far gone! No wonder I ended up as a dog. And yet — all the time I couldn't help thinking about the things Fella had said, and how exactly it all fitted in with what I'd been feeling for so long. What sort of a life had I got lined up anyway? All stress and work and doing things because you're supposed to and because you have to have a good job and neh neh neh neh neh. And the way everyone had fought so hard to stop me doing the things I wanted to! At least a dog can do what she wants.

Terry lay next to me, a stinking heap under the blanket, stunned with alcohol. Was I wasting my time? Maybe I should stop groaning away about what I'd lost, and enjoy what I had instead, like Fella said. But that thought made me despair — to give up my family, my friends, my life. Everything I used to think was such a pain now seemed like the only things worth having. I wanted them back so much, I felt I would burst. I knew then that I'd do anything to get back on the human track again.

I whimpered and cried, and tried to utter some phrases, but my mouth was all wrong. The hours passed, crawling by like a procession of beetles off into the night. Then, when the sky was just beginning to turn pale, I heard a bark nearby. I jumped to my feet to greet Fella and Mitch.

I was so happy to have some company, even the company of dogs. At least they understood me. I lowered my head and licked my lips as we said hello with our eager noses. One thing about dogs – they know how to greet someone. It's not so much scratch and sniff as sniff and lick – as soon as you see someone, you just gotta know what they taste like!

When we were done we licked our lips around our sweet dog-scent and lay all together in a heap in the dirt next to Terry, stinking in his blanket.

'I used to lie there by his side, watching over him, just like you,' said Mitch. He saw me looking and nodded. 'Oh, yeah, we've all done it – even Fella.'

'He's good with a dog, Terry, I'll say that,' panted Fella. 'It won't get you anywhere though, doll. He's done all the good to you he can.'

'You don't know that,' said Mitch. 'He didn't turn me back, and he didn't turn you back, but there've been others.'

'What others?' I asked. 'Who got turned? Tell me!'

'Well, there was Joby. He used to sell the *Big Issue* in Withington for a while. Brown hair, going grey. He wore big blue glasses all taped up.'

'I know him, yes,' I barked excitedly. 'What happened?'

'He stole some beer,' said Mitch, and shrugged.

'Same as me! I knocked it out of his hand.'

'Mess with ma beer, you're a dog,' hissed Fella.

'He lived with Terry for weeks after he got turned, wouldn't talk to us, barked like a maniac when we went anywhere near him,' Mitch went on. 'In denial, see. Couldn't take it. You never saw him more than three feet away from Terry, staring pathetically up at him for weeks, if not months. Then, one day, he got turned back.'

'You don't know that,' said Fella. 'You never saw him.'

'I did better than see him, I smelt him.'

Fella snorted irritably. 'Maybe, but so what? Do you think it made him happier? Better off? What did he have? A handful of *Big Issues*, a place in the refuge if he was lucky. He could have licked his way to heaven! Yeah – he was never gonna be a dog, he lacked the courage of his own convictions.' Fella was watching me as he spoke, but I didn't have the heart for any more debate about dog versus person and I looked away. He tossed his head slightly – a strangely human gesture – and sat down again. 'It's your choice,' he said. He yawned widely and snapped his jaws shut. 'But you don't have to be a pet all the time. Get Terry to stay in the refuge when you can and then you can have a night out with the pack. I bet you used to like nights out, eh?'

I coughed and looked away. I used to live for nights out, but that was behind me now. If I ever got back among my own kind, I was going to work hard, settle down, do the right thing. If that's what it took, that's what I was going to do. Whether I liked it or not.

'Yeah, he's right about that, you really should,' barked Mitch. 'A night out with the dogs – that's worth dying for. And it's good for Terry, too,' he added. 'He needs to sleep indoors, on a bed, but he won't go in the refuge when he has a dog with him. They don't allow dogs. You'll see in the morning what a night on the streets does to a man.'

There was a pause as we all three looked at the heap of Terry. Was this a magician? He stank of beer and piss. When I was a girl, I wouldn't have even imagined spending the night curled up with a such a creature. Now, all I wanted was to feel his hand upon my back.

Fella was going into one of his acts. He stood up on his hind legs, put his paw on his hip and leered down at Terry.

'Hey, sweetheart, have you got any *time* for me,' he said in a high-pitched whine, like a cartoon film star making a come on. 'Y'know, you're just so sexy. Ooooh, so sexy, ah kin hardly hold myself back. Are you *listening* to me? I say, are you *listening* to me?' But of course Terry just lay in his blanket, grunting and snoring like an alcoholic pig. Fella looked down at him in disgust and then went into his giant rat act. It was the first time I saw it, and I never made up my mind whether it was funny or scary. He drew up his lip so his front teeth stood out, doubled his legs underneath so they looked really short, stretched his thin, whippy tail out behind him and went sniffing and creeping across the ground. He did already look a bit like a rat, with his long nose and bulgy eyes. He went sniffing and licking his lips all round Terry's face, as if he was going to eat bits off him. It was so realistic it made me screech.

'Jesus, that's horrible – ugh, that's *really* horrible!' I yelped.

'He did it once to this couple who caught us kipping in a house they were thinking of buying. No sale that day, I can tell you! They had Rentokil round there for weeks afterwards,' spluttered Mitch.

Fella made me laugh, but he scared me too. I didn't want to listen to him going on any more. I'd been on the wild side long enough – see where it'd got me! I turned to Mitch.

'What about you? Tell me your story. How did you get turned?' I begged.

Mitch looked at Fella to see what he was up to, but Fella stood back up and stretched.

'Go ahead, tell her. We've got time,' he said. He yawned, lay down on his side and closed his eyes as if he was about to go to sleep. Mitch sat down and scratched, like he always did when he had a story to tell. Then he stopped and gazed out towards the road, as if he was listening to the cars and lorries and buses going past, while he gathered his thoughts.

'You know, I can hardly remember it,' he said at last. 'Trauma, I suppose.'

'Maybe you just can't be bothered any more,' yawned Fella. 'It was all you talked about for months. The Day I Became a Dog.'

'It was a big event.'

'A turning point, you might say,' said Mitch, and both dogs laughed down their noses.

'After school. In the Tesco car park at Didsbury,' Fella reminded him.

'I can remember where, I just can't remember what. Thursday afternoon. I'd just done a shop.' Mitch paused, leg hovering in the air next to his ear. 'It was those girls wasn't it, those Year 10s?'

'With Terry.'

'That's right. They were making a hell of a racket, laughing and whooping and screeching. I went over to see what the problem was.'

'What problem?' said Fella. 'They were having a good time.' He grinned, and licked his chops. 'I was watching, I saw it all,' he told me.

'Terry was grinning and they were laughing, but you could see they weren't comfortable,' went on Mitch. 'They stopped giggling as soon as they saw me. I taught them at school, see,' he explained to me. 'Terry asked them who I was, and one of them told him but that didn't stop him. I think he thought at first I was a parent or something, but when he knew I was a teacher, he just carried right on.'

'Right on what?'

'Well, he was just being filthy. In a really unsuitable

way to carry on with a group of girls. They were only about fifteen.'

'Like what?' I asked.

'Just — filthy,' repeated Mitch. 'I don't know what he'd been saying to them, but he started on me, then. Asking me what it was like teaching a bunch of attractive girls like that. Did I ever get to feel them up? Of course the girls were killing themselves laughing. Which ones had I snogged? Then he tried to put his arm over one of their shoulders. The girl shrugged him off. Totally unsuitable. I had to intervene, didn't I?'

'They were OK. What harm was he going to do them, Thursday afternoon, people everywhere? They were having a laugh,' said Fella.

'He could have turned them into dogs.'

'You didn't know that.'

'What did you do?' I asked.

'Well, I told the girls to go away, and warned Terry that I might have to call the police if he didn't behave himself. The trouble is, the girls didn't respond, didn't respond at all. It was so humiliating. One of them — Amanda Cabot, she was the ringleader. She got really cheeky. She started telling Terry that he was quite right, I was a dirty old man, and I was always trying it on with all the girls, and all these horrible things I was supposed to have done with various women teachers at school. I told her off of course . . . '

'"What's up with you, it's out of school hours, isn't it? Why don't you just mind your own business, we're having a private conversation,"' said Fella, in a high-pitched girly voice, in a Manchester accent.

'Exactly.'

'So what happened?'

'So I lost my temper and tried to grab hold of Terry. The girls started threatening *me* with the police. Me! I was their teacher! Then I made my fatal mistake. I grabbed his beer out of his hands.'

'It's the beer every time,' said Fella. 'Terry should have a big sign on him. WARNING! DO NOT REMOVE BEER. DANGER OF CANIFICATION.'

'Yeah, every time. You can kick him in the teeth and he thinks he deserves it. Spit on him and he doesn't care. Take his beer and he's as fierce as a tiger. Anyway, next thing, I'm a dog. Bang, on the floor barking indignantly. And that was that.'

'It was the most amazing thing you ever saw,' put in Fella. 'Oh, yeah, I was watching the whole thing,' he said. 'I knew Mitch . . .'

'What, were you friends?' I asked.

'No, I used to go to the same school, Parrs Wood.'

'That was my school, too!' I barked. That meant I might even have met them, but there were so many teachers and so many students, I had no idea which ones they'd been.

'Fella – well, he was Simon in those days – was one of the best students we ever had,' said Mitch, which took me by surprise. 'A stars in Art, Physics and Maths.'

'He has a brain?' I asked, sarcastically.

Fella took no notice of me. 'I saw him turn into a dog, and I was just — I dunno, sorry for Mitch of course, but at the same time I was so pleased. It was partly because I realised at that moment — yeah! A dog! That's what I want to be! And I was jealous of him, you know? I thought, You lucky bastard! It was such a relief because I was stuck in that old human way of thinking, like, you have to know everything, you have to understand everything. You know what I mean? Everyone has to be right. It was such an effort, being right all the time about everything, doing the right thing. And now at last, here it was, something that was utterly impossible, something no one could explain — something useless and haphazard and crazy, and it was such a relief! I just *knew* there was more going on in the world than met the eye. It was a revelation to me. You know, you watch the cars going up and down the street, you watch the sun coming up each morning. Plants growing, people thinking and feeling. I used to think you could explain everything if you just work it out — but now, I realised that actually I knew nothing at all. I thought — yes! Here it is. This is the big one. I'd never thought about it but now I knew I'd been expecting something like this to happen for years!

'I just had to get involved,' he went on. 'I thought, OK, I hadn't got a clue what was happening, but Terry had obviously done something to the man, so I went over and started shouting at him. "How dare you? How dare you turn that man into a dog? Turn him back this instant!

Who do you think you are?" ' Fella giggled at the memory of his telling Terry off like that. 'And you know what? It might have worked. Terry was so appalled that anyone had the temerity to mention what he'd just done. I mean, plenty of people must have seen it over the years, but I think they just must have kept their mouths shut or blocked it off or something. And there was I shouting it out at the top of my voice! I really think he might have done something about it – anything just to shut me up, you know – but those girls got in on it. One of them chucked a stone at him. He'd picked up his can, which Mitch had dropped when he lost his hands. It still had some beer left in it, but when the stone hit him on the neck, he cried out and dropped it. The trouble was, for some reason, he thought I'd done it. I was expecting that girl to get dogged, but it wasn't her – it was me. One minute I was standing there shouting, the next, I was on all fours barking. The girls ran off, screaming. I jumped at Terry and bit him hard on the leg. He fell over, and I tell you, I'd have had his throat out. I had him down, I had my teeth clamped on his shirt front and I was snarling, "Turn me back, you bastard, turn me back or I'll eat you!" but then some people came running over and I had to run off.'

'You weren't so keen on being a dog at first, then?' I asked.

'Actually, you know, I think I was, but it just took a few days to sink in. Right at that moment, I just thought he'd done this to me without my permission. That's

94

what I was cross about.'

I looked at Mitch, who'd lain down dejectedly. 'What about you? How did you react?' I asked.

Mitch sighed. 'I was devastated. I still am. I think I could almost get used to it if it wasn't for just one thing. My family.' He gulped and raised his head. 'Every day I go to see if I can catch a glimpse of my wife and children. I miss them. I'd give anything for just one night back in my family home, with my wife by my side and my two boys curled up in front of the TV, together again. I miss them so much.'

Mitch whined again, and laid down his head. Fella and I went over to lick his face and sniff under his tail to try and cheer him up.

'Come on,' said Fella. 'It's just what happens. We've all lost something – everything, in one way. But look what you've gained! Think about the fun we had earlier tonight! Eh? Now, what about that?' Mitch's tail wagged and he lifted up his head.

'What have you been doing? Do you have masters, too?' I asked them, but both growled and shook their heads.

'Masters! Who'd want to be owned by one of those things?' said Fella.

'We look after ourselves,' said Mitch proudly. 'Did you know that dogs are nocturnal? It's only people who've trained us to trot about during the day, because it suits them. But in the wild, we like the night. What could be better than to run in cover of darkness. To run with the pack!'

'A pack?' I barked excitedly. 'How many are there?'

'Well, others come along most nights, but they're just dogs. We're waiting for more members. We're waiting for you, baby,' said Fella, and he stretched his lips into a terrible parody of a grin, that looked more a snarl on him and made me raise my hackles.

'We were on the trail of a fox tonight,' said Mitch suddenly. 'Nearly got him too.'

'All the way up the railway line as far as Hulme,' said Fella.

'Then he took off across the streets and into the park, us on his tail. We gave tongue...'

'...barked like bastards, he means. Ran through the park right on his stinking heels. Then he turned off...'

'Dived into the side streets. We followed, but then...'

'Then what?' I asked.

'We smelt a bitch on heat and got distracted,' said Fella.

Both dogs found somewhere to scratch while I had a think about that.

'And did you...?'

'Nah, she was locked up,' said Mitch casually. 'There was half the dogs in Manchester barking round her yard.'

My aunt had a spaniel bitch that was on heat once and she didn't dare take her into the park in case she ran off with a dog. I was a bitch. I thought about that phrase — bitch on heat.

'How often does, er, a bitch get on heat?'

'Few times a year.' Fella winked at me. 'You're gonna love it, baby,' he told me. 'And so am I!' I growled at him to show him – Don't mess with me, brother!

I had a lick down there just to check that there was nothing different, when a thought occurred to me. 'Hunting – hey! Did you ever get a cat?'

'Cats?' said Mitch in offended terms, but Fella was up and wagging.

'Oh, yeah, I'd love to get a cat – and I could do it with you, baby! This old bugger won't touch them.'

'Cats!' said Mitch again, in disgust. 'You can't eat them, they run on the roof. Don't bother with cats. It lacks . . . ' he paused, looking for the word. I cringed down, ashamed of myself.

'Dignity,' said Mitch.

'I suppose,' I said.

Fella groaned. 'Save dignity for the bloody old human race!' he barked. 'I wanna get a cat!' But all I could think about was being human again, and I closed my eyes and shook my head and tried not to think about it.

We sat for a while, all three dogs together, until there was barking some way off, and in a second, without a word, Fella and Mitch were on their feet and gone like the wind.

I was alone with my master again.

FIVE

Terry woke up as the sun crept round the building and lit up the yard where we slept. His face was swollen, his breath was foul, but I was so happy to see him, I licked him into the morning. He groaned, took my face in his hands and kissed my nose. I could feel the cold of the ground in him. For the first time ever that morning I thought I was lucky to be a dog. I could sleep out and wake up refreshed, but the man . . . ! It looked as if the Earth was killing him.

He pulled himself upright and took a can out of his pocket.

'Good morning to you, Lady,' he told me. He took a drink, and as the liquid hit his stomach, he retched. I think he was sick, but if he was, he managed to hold it and swallow it back. He waited a little before taking another little sip, and the same thing happened. Drinking in little sips like this, Terry gradually forced enough booze down his throat to be able to face the day.

'Now then,' he said. 'Now then.' He stood up shakily, patted his pocket and came up with a few scraps of bread he'd saved for my breakfast. He stood grimly over me while I wolfed them down and sat up, looking for more.

'We have to earn our keep today, Lady,' he told me. He sat down and finished his can. It was like watching a piece of old machinery slowly coming to life as the oil crept round its gears, or watching the sun warming up a beetle that had stayed out too late at night. When the can was empty he got down on his knees by me and kissed me and patted me and stroked me and made such a fuss of me that I thought he lived only for me. And me – I was so grateful and so happy! Mitch was right, Terry really knew how to treat a dog! As it went on I became happier and happier until I was yelping and whining and crouching in excitement. Then he stood back up and stretched himself, and set about teaching me how to earn my keep.

Terry didn't have any great ambitions for me. He just wasted me, really. I could have walked or danced or talked about the weather, or discussed 'EastEnders' – you name it! When you have a girl's brain in the body of a dog, everything is a miracle. But all Terry wanted me to do was learn how to say one simple phrase. He found it hilarious. It took him five minutes getting it out, he was laughing so much.

'Thanks, mate!' he burst out at last. That was it.

'Jesus, what do you think, eh, Lady? Isn't it totally bloody brilliant? Eh? Eh? Oh, God, I'll kill myself!' he howled. He kept breaking into giggles as he explained. I had to say it whenever someone dropped money into the dog bowl. 'Just when they drop money in, mind, not before,' insisted Terry. 'It's a sort of reward for them, you see,' he told me. 'God, they'll kill themselves laughing!' And he fell around laughing himself, all over again. God knows why. I couldn't see the joke. Maybe it was the idea of giving people a reward; maybe it was just the talking dog, I don't know. I mean! Thanks, mate? Was that it? All those boring years being educated and learning about igneous rocks and square roots and what the Romans did on their days off, and all I was going to do was say thank you nicely! But I couldn't argue; Master knows best. And who knows, maybe he was right. I had to spend half the morning learning to get my stiff dog's mouth around just those two words.

By mid morning I made a passable imitation of human speech, and we went off to try it out.

Terry took me further down the Oxford Road to the University. As we walked along he explained to me that students were suckers for a laugh. 'They'll laugh at anything,' he said, 'and they're too dopey to think it's anything more than a trick. Mean, though,' he added. A few people glanced to see a man chatting familiarly to his dog in the street, but it was only a poor man with no home and too much beer inside him. How could they know I understood every word? After the first glance, they carried on. Nothing unusual there.

'We must find the right spot. Every trade has its skills,' said Terry, and he went off on a long explanation of the advantages of begging at railway stations, arts centres, cinemas, shops and cash machines. To hear him go on you'd think he had a PhD in the subject, but at last we got ourselves settled down in between Abdul's and the Lloyd's Bank cash machine on the Oxford Road. Terry put the dog bowl out, sat himself down, and we waited for our first customer.

And waited and waited. Students came and went, but no money.

'Selfish little shites,' growled Terry. 'But you wait until they catch on, the money will come raining down. You'll be eating steak tonight, Lady. Good girl!' He rubbed my head and I wagged my tail and tried to look cute, but cute don't catch no carrots. Finally Terry got fed up waiting and started going through his own pockets, looking for a coin.

'We need something to start 'em off,' he told me. He got out a two pence, all he had in the world, and dropped it in the bowl as a couple of girls walked past. 'Go on,' he hissed.

'Thanks, mate,' I said. One of the girls glanced down at me, then at Terry.

'What?' she said.

'It wasn't me, it was the dog. Here . . . ' He picked the coin up. 'She always says thank you. Although 2p – not even a cocktail sausage for that,' he said, and started giggling and blushing at the same time.

The girl scrowled. 'I didn't put any money in.'

'Oh, someone must have.'

'Well, how does she say thank you, then?'

'Try her,' said Terry, and he wrapped his arms round his legs and grinned like a madman.

The other girl was getting impatient. 'Come on, let's go,' she said.

'I thought that dog said something.'

'What?'

'Thanks, mate. It said, "Thanks, mate."'

'It's a she,' said Terry.

The girl slapped her bag and laughed. 'She can't have . . .'

'Try her! Try her!' insisted Terry. So the girl did as she was told. She dug out ten pence, dropped it in . . .

'Thanks, mate!' I said loudly.

'Oh my God!'

'Did you hear that!'

'Oh my God!'

'Make her do it again,' begged the second girl, who couldn't believe her ears.

'She needs some money first.'

The girls rummaged about in their bags and came up with more coins. 'Minimum of ten pence,' insisted Terry.

'She did it for two pence before,' said one of the girls, but her friend told her not to be mean. A ten pence dropped in.

'Thanks, mate.'

Another.

'Thanks, mate.'

Another.

'Thanks, mate!' I barked, and they fell around roaring

with laughter, just as Terry said they would.

'Thanks, mate, did you hear her? She says thanks!' spluttered the girls. And the fuss was attracting attention. Other people stopped, a couple of boys, another girl...

'Listen!' said the first one. 'It's a talking dog, listen!' She chucked in another ten pence.

'Thanks, mate!' I barked. And it was the same thing all over again. At first they didn't believe they'd heard right and had to put more money in to be sure; then they killed themselves laughing and had to put more in to get more laughs, and then they wanted to try it on their friends. Everyone wanted a go!

'Thanks, mate!' I barked. 'Thanks, mate,' I growled. I shouted it, hissed it, whimpered it, cried it, growled it. I was a star! The money piled up, the crowd grew and grew, Terry laughed until the tears ran down his face and his eyes turned red.

'Thanks, mate, thanks, thanks, thanks!' On it went. We were a circus! We were a funfair! It was glorious, I never saw Terry so happy. And me – I was the centre of attention. I loved every minute of it.

And then suddenly someone said, 'What's the crap, then?'

A big bloke, head shaved bare, neck like a tank. It wasn't warm but he wore a vest even so. He stood staring down at Terry as if he was a piece of shit on his shoe while the others explained. He waited until they'd done, watched me perform. Then he said, 'You stole that dog, didn't you?'

'She's my dog!' wailed Terry in a high voice. He put an arm round me and cringed away from the big student.

'Oh, leave him alone, George,' shouted someone, but George was just getting going.

'Look at his face, he's done something. He never trained that dog to do that. He nicked it. You nicked it, didn't you?'

'She's mine,' shouted Terry, getting to his feet and preparing to run. And already the crowd was turning against him. One look at Terry and you knew that George was right. He obviously had something to be guilty about.

The big student reached down and snatched the string tied around my neck. 'I'll just take her round the nick, see what the old filth have to say about it, eh? If I was you, I'd make myself scarce.'

Terry was on his feet and backed away out of reach, where his courage came back a bit. He pointed at the big bloke and shouted, 'Get him, Lady.'

I didn't need telling twice. I jumped for him. I could have gone for his arm or his leg, but I'd have got a boot for my trouble – I was never a big dog. His face was too high, so I did what I've always done in a fight: I went straight for his knackers.

Bull's-eye! I dived in nose first right into his pants and I bit. I bit hard. I got the whole goose and her eggs in my jaws and I clenched right up. It was brilliant! The crowd howled, George roared and spun round. I hung a bit longer, swinging with him and growling like a fiend, before I finally let go.

'Me knackers!' howled George. He clutched himself and bent his knees like an old lady who'd wet her pants. The crowd were howling with laughter, with us again every step of the way.

'She's knackered his knackers!' someone shouted.

'Rather her than me!'

'Not much meat there!'

The crowd loved it. George, still groaning, started to stumble away. I ran to Terry, he seized my string and we set off. Behind us the students hooted with laughter as we ran round the corner and out of sight.

Terry dragged me out of town right up past Rusholme before he felt able to settle down. We kept stopping to laugh.

'Oh, God, the way you were holding on and growling! He'll have nads like a pair of burgers!' groaned Terry. To celebrate, we found a butcher and Terry bought me two pounds of rump steak. Two pounds! I stuffed myself, but poor Terry, after much humming and haa-ing, bought himself a bottle of whiskey. He carried it out with a serious look on his face, and headed straight for a derelict old garden he knew of. There, hidden out of sight, he opened his bottle.

'It's goodbye for now, Lady,' he told me. He looked grim. Whiskey was serious business. 'You might as well take the afternoon off. I'll be all right here,' he told me. He raised the bottle and drank.

Well, he was right. I waited a bit, but within the hour the poor sod was out cold. I sat down by his side, determined to wait and stand guard, but I couldn't bear to sit out the whole day. I'd been sitting all night and all morning. A dog needs exercise. I set off for a wander.

My tail was going bananas as I rounded the corner and headed into Platt Fields park. The pavement was alive; my nose was an eye that sees into the past. I speeded up. Oh, I was in love with Terry, but to run and sniff and feel my ears catching sounds out of the air! But what do you know? Only a dog could understand what I mean.

I ran into the park like a wild animal and raced across the grass. It was spring, everything was going. For an hour or so, I was in doggy heaven. I chased the ducks and the squirrels, I snuffed the scents of half a million dogs, I rolled and panted and laughed. It was the first time I had given myself so completely to scents – my nose just took over. Rabbits and squirrels and rats and mice – I followed them and lost them and found another one, went back and across and to and fro. I didn't catch a thing, but who cares? Just to run and sniff and be alive was all I cared about!

I was so wrapped up in my nose that I don't think I saw a thing for – who knows? Hours, maybe. Dogs don't watch the clock. But then, while I was lapping water from the lake, I looked up and a face stopped me in my tracks.

It was a girl. She was talking to a boy who I sort of knew as well, but although they were so familiar, I couldn't place them. My nose had taken over so much that for a moment I couldn't work out who they were or what they were saying. They all looked the same, like different types of animal do. They almost made me laugh, with their funny flat faces twisting and wriggling about on their heads in that strange way.

I shook my head, trying to see like a person sees. I was walking towards them, staring at them so hard that they noticed me and began to look suspiciously at me. I shook my head again – and it all came back to me. It was Annie, my old best friend – Annie and her bloke, Little-Willie. I was so pleased to see her, I let out a little woof of surprise and pleasure and went bounding over to say hello.

'What's that want?'

'I dunno, I've never seen it before.'

'Good girl!' Nervously, Annie stopped and patted me. I was so grateful for the touch of her fingers that I rolled without thinking onto my back, begging for her to tickle my tummy.

They both laughed. I was so pleased to see them! I wanted to show off. I was having such good fun running about in the park. I thought how much better off I was than them. I had no exams to worry about, no lifetime of work or kids to bring up or any of that stuff. No responsibilities. I could run faster, hear better, smell better. I could sleep on the pavement and not get cold, walk all day and not get tired... Who wants to be human, I thought? I began to jump about and run around, showing them how easy life was for me.

They stood and watched me for a bit, smiling at me, then they turned round and walked away.

I was offended! They just turned their backs on me as if I was of no importance at all. I woofed and went after them. The boy turned round and I jumped up, putting my paws on his chest. He laughed and banged my sides, and I rolled down on the ground for him as well, so that he could tickle my tummy, too.

Annie laughed. 'She's a bit of a slut, isn't she?' she said.

You know what? That just pissed me off. How dare she? I was only being friendly — how did that make me a slut? OK, I knew she was just joking, but she was always like that, Annie — always so superior, always knowing best, always so certain that the way she was going about things was right. I got up and looked at her staring down at me with a wry little smile on her face as if she was so far above me that I barely counted at all — as if everyone in the world could see how wrong I was and how right she was.

She pointed at me staring at her and laughed. 'Doesn't she look funny?' she said.

'"Ha ha ha! Doesn't she look funny!"' I sneered sarcastically, but I don't think she understood a word.

For a moment we stood there, her looking at me and me looking at her, and I thought of all the times she'd done better than me at just about everything. She always did better than me – at school, at games, with boys. Her boyfriends were always more caring, more grown-up, more responsible. Better boyfriends. I always ended up with the ones who feel you up and then dump you. But actually, when I thought about it, it wasn't her doing better at all – it was her just *assuming* that she was doing better. It was her assuming that the things she did well were better than the things I did well – that school work was more important than knowing how to enjoy yourself, or that games were even worth doing in the first place. I mean, who cares if you can put a ball in a net quicker than someone else? Or that the caring boys were better than the careless ones. That sort of thing. And she'd had me fooled! Because all the time, I'd been assuming the same thing. That was the really awful thing about it – that for all those years I'd been assuming that I wanted to be like her but just wasn't good enough at it. You know what I mean? As if I was some sort of sub-rate Annie Turner. And then, as soon as I started doing things differently, as soon as I started doing things like *I* wanted to do them, she was the first one to think that I was wrong all over again and an even bigger failure than before. It made me so cross – but at the same time I wanted us to be friends again the way we used to be.

I just wanted to fool around and make her laugh and get at her at the same time. I started pretending to be Little-Willie. I got up on my hind legs. They stared in amazement. Then I walked over to a tree, just about staying upright, put my paws down to my you-know-what and looked down as if I was peeing.

'Ugh, look at it!'

'That's weird. That's sick!'

'Do you think it's all right?'

'Watch out! It's looking at us!'

They began to back off, but I hadn't finished yet. I started patting down round where my willy would be if I was a boy.

'Oh, God, it's gone! My willy's fallen off,' I cried. I started searching about, patting the hair, looking around, crawling about on the floor, yelping and muttering to myself all the time.

'It's gone! It's dropped off! Has anyone seen my willy, I can't find it, it's only a teeny tiny weenie willy, but it's the only one I've got! Help! I'm not Little-Willie any more! I'm No-Knob!'

I don't know about them, but it was making me laugh. I fell to the ground howling with laughter, but Annie and Toby weren't amused. Looking back, I can hardly blame them. I must have looked completely crazy, dancing about like that on my hind legs. And of course, they couldn't make out a word I was saying, it must have just been a series of weird growls and moans and howls. When I looked over at them, their faces had drained completely of blood. Annie half hid behind Little-Willie and they began to back off.

'Don't go!' I cried, but my calls were a hideous parody of barking and speaking. Suddenly Annie screamed, turned and ran. I was appalled. I only wanted to make her laugh! Well, that's not quite true, I was being spiteful too – but I wanted her to know me! I wanted to be friends! Suddenly I realised how horribly wrong the whole thing must have seemed to them. My mood of just seconds ago changed utterly. Now I was terrified. I ran after them, calling out their names. 'Toby! Toby! Don't you know me?' I begged. I jumped up at him, but he screamed in fear and kicked out.

Both of them were screaming and running now, and I could see other people running to help, some of them shouting angrily at me. I meant no harm – but it was too late now. As far as they were concerned I was some mad dog, turning savage. My life was in danger! I turned and ran away across the grass as fast as my legs could carry me. When I was out of sight, I dived into some shrubbery to hide. I was so overcome with emotion that I was shaking. I wasn't mad! I wasn't savage! Were they really going to put me down just because I took the piss? Didn't any of them understand? I wanted to cry, but I had no tears. I was a dog. No one would ever know me again.

As I cringed in the shrubbery, fearful for my life, I had a sudden, desperate need for human company. My family! I was gripped with a terrible panic that I'd never be able to communicate with them ever again, that they'd always see me like this – as something revolting and mad that ought to be destroyed. I hadn't even thought about them for days, but now I was desperate just to glimpse them – just to reassure myself that they were still there, that they still remembered me even if they could never recognise me ever again.

Forgetting even about the danger to my life, I dashed out of my hiding place and raced off across the grass. I had to see them! I had to make sure they were all right!

I was already thinking so much like a girl again that I was amazed at how quickly my feet took me back home – through the park, out opposite Sainsbury's and then I just shot off behind Withington and into the estate. Past the cars, past the roads – bang! – and there was my house, sitting like something in a picture I'd seen long ago and then forgotten.

Down went my tail. I crouched on the pavement and whined. What could I do to get back everything I'd lost? Family, friends, a lifetime before me – all gone. I remembered Fella's words – 'A dog's days are short...'

Carefully, tenderly almost, I nosed open the gate, crossed the front lawn to the window, put my feet on the sill and looked into the front room.

It was all so, so familiar – the settee, the TV in the corner, the carpet, the rug, the cushions. If only I could jump in through the window and be a girl again before I landed on my feet. Where was everyone? Adam would be at school, but what about Mum? She'd have finished by now.

I ran round the back and looked in through the French windows at the back, but there was no one in. I hung around in the back garden for a while, hiding under the hedge, until at last there was a noise at the front. Quickly, silently, I ran to stick my head around the corner – and there she was with her key in the lock. My heart just leaped for joy.

My mum! Isn't it funny – I forgot in a second how she'd betrayed me and failed to know who I was. I forgot all my angry thoughts about her – of course she loves me! And of course I loved her. I may get cross and say horrible things, but in my heart, I never doubted it for a second.

I was just in time to see her push the door open and go inside, and it was all I could do to stop myself barking with joy. My own mum! I knew her, but she didn't know me – how could she? I ducked back in case she turned round and saw me. I didn't want to scare her – I couldn't bear her to be scared of me.

I went back under the hedge and tried to work out what to do, but in the end there was nothing. They would never know me or accept me as I was. I hung around the house all afternoon and all evening in the end. I just wanted to see them even though I couldn't be a part of the family again – not yet, anyway. I wanted to remind myself of what I really was. I saw my mum on her own in the sitting room sipping a cup of tea. I listened at the back door while she cooked dinner. The radio was playing a silly little song – you remember it, 'Little Men' by the Stereo Pop – and she sang along.

'Oh, the little men come, one two three,
One for you and two for me,
Oh, the little men wear silly hats,

Always pointed, never flat,' she sang.

I forgot myself and tried to join in. Of course, she stopped singing at once when she heard my racket, and I had to run and hide away under the hedge again while she came to look at what had made such an ugly noise.

I was horrified all over again. We used to sing that song together, it had been in the charts for weeks. Now it scared her to hear me. But then I got angry again. I mean – she was my mother and I couldn't even sing along to her songs. I couldn't even show myself to her or she started screeching and yelling. I lay under that bush growling away to myself under my breath – but I was too exhausted by emotion to keep it up, and I soon got depressed and just lay there, licking my paws and whining to myself.

Later on, Adam came home from school and plumped himself as usual in front of the TV. Mum made him a sandwich and a cup of tea. I watched him eat it through the sitting room window, ducking and diving whenever he looked up. It was hard because cars or people kept going past and I had to hide from them too; but I had my ears and nose to help me there. I spent the whole evening tormenting myself like that. Later still, Julie came by. As soon as she opened the door, my mum came out and threw her arms around her and they both burst into tears.

I was so relieved to see them cry. Isn't that selfish of me? Although it had been comforting in a way to see everything looking so normal, it was really upsetting because it looked as if me disappearing had made no difference at all. I suppose I should have been happy that I hadn't wrecked their lives, but when I saw them crying their hearts out, I was pleased.

'I don't think we'll ever see her again, Julie,' said my mum. At the same moment, Adam appeared behind them in the hall and guess what? There were tears in his eyes, too. My whole family weeping for me. I felt my heart overflow. I'd thought I was just a problem for them, but all the time they loved me, even Adam who never said a friendly word. They loved me so much that their lives would never be the same again without me. Unable to help myself, a low howling moan escaped my lips. Mum looked over Julie's shoulder and saw me.

'It's that dog – the mad one – look!' she said. Everyone turned round. I yipped at them, but I had no words, no tears, nothing. I ran off, tail tucked in, body low. Behind me the door slammed. All I could do for those who loved me was to take myself away, and all they wanted was to have me back in their arms!

In the dark, wet Manchester night I roamed the streets not knowing what to do next. But in the end there was only one thing to do – I went back to Terry. He had done this to me, but what other hope was there for me to get my life back? Of course, there was always Fella and Mitch – but I needed people, and Terry was the only one who'd have me.

I found him early the next morning wandering about in front of Blockbusters in Ladybarn. His face lit up when he saw me, and he got down on his knees to hold me and clutch my ears and rub my face. I was so glad to see him!

'You gorgeous girl, where have you been? Off on your adventures? And you came home, you good good girl, you came home!' He wept with joy, and I admit I did too – or I would have done if I could have. Then he slipped the string around my neck and led me up the road towards Levenshume.

So my life passed on, day after day. We would wake up each morning where he'd passed out the night before – among the bins behind a row of shops, or in an old car park, or a shop doorway or a building site. We travelled around from place to place – Northenden, Withington, Didsbury, Ladybarn, sometimes around the town centre, Rusholme, all around south Manchester. By the evening he was senseless with drink, but he always managed to make it to somewhere that would keep the rain off our heads, and made sure we had some cardboard or a bit of old blanket to rest on. Each morning he woke up slowly, sipping carefully at his Special Brew to try and make sure as much of it stayed down as possible, until he was able to face the day. Then we would be off to make our living.

Over the next week he taught me to say various other words and phrases as the money rattled into the dog bowl. 'Sausages,' worked well – it had everyone in roars of laughter, although it made me hungrier than ever having to say that delicious word over and over again.

One man actually dropped sausages into the bowl as a joke, which pleased me no end but it made Terry cross, because it was his joke and the man was stealing it.

After lunch, the drinking would begin in earnest. Sometimes we hung around with other tramps and alcoholics, but my Terry was a jealous Terry, and mostly we stayed on our own. He often talked to me as he drank away the afternoons, just as he must once have talked to Fella and Mitch and who knows how many others? There were endless stories about the countless children's homes he'd been in and out of and the lives he'd destroyed with his terrible gift. He'd been married once. Oh yes – had a job packing in a warehouse, a wife, a small pretty girl, to hear him, who gave him a daughter he loved to death.

'But I was jealous,' he told me. 'Jealous as hell of both of them, and I turned them both into bitches one day just because her dinner came before mine. She was only two. They ran off together into the streets behind my house and I never saw them again, although I went out every night with a bowl of meat and called and wept for them to come back to me. Everyone goes away, Lady. And you will too, eh, girl? When poor old Terry becomes too boring for you to bear any more...'

And I licked his face and made silly promises, but we both knew what he said was true. How could any relationship work when one partner was so full of booze so much of the time? If only he could give up the drink, dry out, get his life together. Then perhaps he could help me become myself again and – who knows? Who knows what would have happened between us? I loved him. I'd have done anything for him. I tried to tell him, and I think he understood what I meant. But I was like a hundred other girls, who like to think they can change the man they love – the man who is ruining your life day by day – into something worthwhile. What you see is what you get. That's what you fell in love with in the first place, you silly bitch. Why expect him to turn into something decent?

'Don't look at me like that!' he used to say. He always drank more when I was in that mood, until his conscience went back to sleep and he was as happy as an insect on a leaf.

Well, what could I do? I loved him and waited for the day when he would find the love in him, or the generosity, or whatever it took to turn me back into Sandra Francy. But I was determined to keep my memories of her alive. I spent hours practising growling and barking human words to myself – the names of my family and friends, catch phrases from my favourite programmes on the telly, things we used to eat for dinner – anything to try and keep my memory alive.

And night after night, Fella and Mitch would come to visit me and try to entice me away from my master to run with the pack. I was tempted. A night out with the dogs! Oh, there were so many promises, so many temptations. Left-overs licked out of spilled wheelie bins! Rats, mice, a fox started out of the railway cutting!

And cats! Oh, to kill to cat! To taste her hot blood! I tried not to let Fella see how excited I was by the thought. It was a lust in me, to taste cat blood. It was right there in my spine and my bark and my blood. Mitch disapproved. He thought we should be above all that. A fox – that was fair game. There were plenty of foxes trotting about the night-time gardens and parks, hunting for scraps in the bins, or for slugs and worms in newly dug gardens. But cats were just scum as far as he was concerned, not worth hunting – something only the dregs would put an effort into killing.

I was ashamed and frightened by my strange desires, and I refused to leave my master's side.

Mitch understood, and encouraged me sometimes to think I might get back to what I was, but Fella was infuriated. 'You're a dog, you need a pack. You've chosen Terry and Terry is a shite pack member to be with. Come with me. I'll show you what pack life is all about,' he growled. Then he winked – a disgusting thing to watch a dog do – and under my fur I could feel myself blushing. I held out, though – I held out for ages. I only gave in when I had no choice.

SIX

Dogs don't count the days. The pavements were warming up and the hedges were scented with baby mice and fledglings trying out their wings. There was the smell of young rabbits all over the Southern Cemetery when I was – well. I'll tell you.

It was morning. Terry and me were by the flower-shop on Copson Street, begging as usual, but I was restless. I kept running up and down the pavement and sniffing at poles instead of sitting on the blanket at Terry's feet, getting in the dough. Somehow, saying 'Cheers, mate,' 'Thanks,' and 'Sausages!' just wasn't doing it for me that morning. Terry kept calling me back, and I did my best, but after a few minutes I'd be whining and running up and down again. In the end he had to tie me up to the bench. I was all over the place. I was forgetting everything. Was it sausages, or thank you, or cheers, mate? Or just a good old bark?

'You need more exercise, I suppose,' muttered Terry to himself. He never took me for a walk. All we did each day was walk from place to place, up and down the streets, and round and round, looking for places to sit, eat, sleep and piss. I kept thinking of Ed, who I used to keep in the house all day. It must have driven him mad!

The air that day was full of dogs. I could smell them everywhere, and every time I caught a whiff I was up, sniffing the air, pulling at the string, barking and yelping like a silly pup.

'What, do you want to escape? Do you want to get put down?' said Terry sternly. He knew what was going on – he must have seen it loads of times before. But even though it was only dogs and not bitches who were making me pull away, I still hadn't picked up on what was happening to me.

And the dogs were noticing me. Well, the ones that mattered anyway. You see dogs everywhere, you'd think there'd be loads to choose from, but you'd be amazed. Half of them are bitches and half the rest of them have had their balls cut off. But there were still some about. There was this big black alsatian went past, and as soon as he saw me he was dragging his owner towards me. He didn't just want to sniff. He was well fit. His owner was a pale, skinny-looking bloke with bad skin and a smell of mint and bones on his breath. He had to drag him back with both hands until he stood on his hind legs. He barked at me and I barked back. He kept looking over his shoulder as he was pulled away down the road. His eyes were empty of any sense but I didn't care. He smelt so good! – I was practically drooling as he disappeared round the corner. Then there was this scatty brown and white mongrel, and it was the same thing with him. Barking, pulling at the lead. Couldn't

121

take his eyes off me! He wasn't as good-looking as the big alsatian, and he smelt of cheese and cheap meat, but in the mood I was in, anything in fur would have done.

Ten minutes later the alsatian came back and this time he was alone. His lead trailed behind him like a piece of torn wool. He bounded right up, great tail swinging, head back, eyes on me, smelling of sex. I called out to him – 'Who are you?' but he didn't have a word in him. He was just a dog – but what a dog! Strong thick tail, high proud head, upright neck, black, black eyes. He made me tremble, he was so beautiful, but at the same time he terrified the life out of me, and I lay on my belly on the ground, licking my lips and grinning, while he tried to dig his nose under my tail.

Terry was terrified. 'Go away! Bad dog! Off, off!' he squeaked. He grabbed hold of my collar and tried to drag me away, then he tried to push my back down to make me sit, and I almost snapped at him, he irritated me so much.

The alsatian's boss came running up to us, grabbed the lead and dragged him off. We were both twisting and barking, trying to wriggle free. Terry was furious. He lifted his hand and began beating me on my back, just in front of my tail, shouting,

'Leave him, leave him, leave him!' I whined and looked up at him in amazement. Terry, hitting me? What for? 'We're earning our money, you silly tart,' he growled. But even before he'd finished I'd forgotten that he ever struck me, and I was twisting about to get free again.

The alsatian disappeared off behind the shoppers, choking on his chain. 'Get her off the street, you idiot!' yelled his owner over his shoulder.

'Where to? Where bloody to?' yelled Terry after him. He had nowhere to take me; the street was all he had. Across the road another dog was barking and whining, trying to drag his owner towards me and Terry decided enough was enough. He twisted the string round his hand, undid the knot on the bench leg and set off up the road, dragging me behind him.

I was stinking with desire: the air was full of the scents of fine dogs. Something had to happen. Terry was livid – he hadn't had his drink and we hadn't earned much. He kept stopping and bringing the string down across my back in fury.

'You stupid little bitch! Bad dog, bad dog!' he yelled. People were watching us. The string was thin, the blows stung only slightly through my fur, but I cringed and crouched in shame. He hurt my neck tugging me up the road.

We staggered down to Burton Road and headed up to East Didsbury. I don't know where Terry was trying to take me. Where in a city like this are there no dogs? Then – well, it had to happen. Half way down Burton Road, I got a scent – Fella and Mitch! Oooh, yes . . . ! I knew they couldn't smell me yet, because we were downwind, but it was just a matter of time. And oh, they stank; they stank of wild dog and raw meat and piss and sex sex sex! As we turned the corner onto

Cavendish Road, I swear I could scent the exact second that they caught the first whiff of who I was and what I wanted. I began whining and pawing the ground, and I think Terry knew what was coming because he stood up straight, holding me on a tight rope and peering around him, trying to see which way they'd come.

I could hear Fella barking long before he came into sight. 'You sniffy, licky, shaggy little bitch!' he yelled. Terry tried to hide. He dodged into a shop but they chucked him out. All the time I was pulling and he was getting more and more angry. He was scaring the life out of me with his curses and his blows, but he had that string wrapped tightly in his hand and he wasn't letting go. He dodged down a side street, breaking into a shuffling run, but of course he was no match for the dogs. He'd just dived into an alleyway to make his last stand when they burst together over the wall like angels.

'You are beautiful!' gasped Mitch.

'Bitch on heat! Bitch on heat!' barked Fella. He hit the ground and jumped back up straight at Terry, who let go of the lead and fell backwards to the ground with the big grey lurcher over him. I was free! I didn't even pause to look at him. I had both dogs sniffing under my tail, running round to lick my mouth, whining and grinning at me. We stood for a minute in the alleyway, greeting and testing each other, while Terry crawled backwards, cringing. Then we turned and ran, ran, ran like the wind – ran like there was no tomorrow, and you know what? There was no tomorrow, not for a bitch like me with two fine dogs on her tail, and the whole city to play with.

'The Southern Cemetery,' barked Mitch, bouncing along by my side, his little legs going like pistons.

'But not you,' growled Fella. 'Back off! Back off!' he yelled. He leaned across and snapped at the smaller dog's neck. At once, Mitch fell back.

'Come with me!' he begged me, but I didn't care. Not about him! It was Fella I wanted. You should have seen him, with his ragged grey fur and his black eyes and his long mouth! I wanted his nose under my tail, I wanted his tongue, I wanted his belly on my back.

'With me, with me, Lady,' Mitch whined. But we were gone. Not far, though – I kept stopping. I couldn't wait! The Southern Cemetery was so far away.

'Here, here, here, now, now, now!' I whined.

'In the road?' Fella laughed.

'Anywhere. Who cares!' I barked.

'We'll get stuck,' he barked. 'You'll see. Come on – do as I say, you'll see why!'

'Me! Me – I'll do it anywhere with you, you gorgeous bitch!' shouted Mitch, and I was ready, I'd have done it with him, I'd have done it with next door's cat I was so horned up. But Fella bullied and begged and chased me across the main road and along the verges, and through the hedges around the cemetery. We ran over the graves. We were in the modern part; there were people walking along the gravel paths, planting little flowers and filling vases and praying, but we had no time for them. I have a memory like a photoflash of a woman on her knees with rubber gloves on and a trowel in her hand, of people's faces turned towards us as they walked along the neat graves.

'Shoo! Shoo!' said the woman on her knees. Mitch was standing nearby watching us jealously. Fella and I ran round each other in circles a few times, then he got behind me and was up, on and in. And – oh! Wow wow wow WOW!...

Is that scent rabbit?

You know what? I was a virgin twice – once as a girl and once as a dog. How many people can say that?

The first time I had sex was with Simon. We were making plans about it for ages – where and when and what contraception and so on. Me and Annie were going to do it as close together as possible. There was a bit of a thing about who would get there first, but the big thing was, we had to do it before we were sixteen. To be a virgin at sixteen – that was the pits as far as we were concerned. It's like, waiting for permission – like your dad's standing at the end of the bed with a stop watch. 'OK, she's coming up for sixteen...5, 4, 3, 2... wait for it...1! Go!' I mean, it's like it's not even your own body when someone else tells you when, know what I mean?

We were planning on doing it properly in a big double bed, but the only double beds we had available belonged to our parents and who wants to christen your sex life in your parents' bed? Sniffing your dad's armpits on the sheets? Ugh! No thanks. On the other hand I didn't want to do it in the back of a car or have a knee trembler up against a tree or anything like that.

Me and Annie spent ages talking about it. Actually, I spent much longer talking about it with Annie than I did with Simon. He had this really annoying idea that it was all my decision. I mean, not like he didn't want to do it, but, like, everything had to be the way I wanted it, like it was going to be some terrible ordeal for me that had to be made as comfortable as possible.

'It's like I'm losing something and you're getting something,' I said.

'No it isn't!' he insisted. But it was.

'It isn't like you're taking advantage of me or anything,' I told him.

'I know, I know, I'm not saying that. Ha, ha! You know me — I just want to get it,' he joked. He was always turning things into jokes when he didn't know what was going on. It didn't half irritate me. I think it was an old-fashioned, sexist way of thinking — as if he was doing something to me, not with me. Like I was his victim, or he was the doctor or something like that. He was being a right bloody little gentleman about it. All he could think about was what I wanted, and making it all right for me, and he couldn't put two thoughts together about how he wanted it to be for him.

In the end we got fed up waiting. Not me and Simon, me and Annie. We thought of all sorts of places. On holiday, in the countryside, in the open, with the sun on our bare skin — but what if someone came along? I kept imagining people hiding in the bushes watching us. I was shy, I wanted to be hidden away. And in the end, you know what? There was nowhere right. You don't have anywhere that's your own when you're fifteen.

We were still putting it off when my sixteenth birthday was only a month or so away. I remember thinking that at this rate, I was going to turn into the dreaded sixteen-year-old virgin unless I ended up shagging Simon on the living room floor while my mum was watching 'EastEnders'. And then, out of the blue, Annie announced that her boyfriend's parents were going away and leaving him alone in the house for the weekend.

'This is it,' she squeaked, and I was furious because she was going to get there first. I was the one who did things first! I was the one who always dived in without thinking about it and just did them, while she was still making plans.

'I'm not diving in, I *have* made plans, we've been talking about it for ages. I'm just taking advantage of the right opportunity,' she told me, which was true. It was my fault for waiting until everything was just right. That's one thing I've learned — don't wait for it to be perfect or you'll wait forever. I mean, you can't be spontaneous and get everything right, can you? In fact, sometimes you can't even get *anything* right, if you're me, anyway. Getting it right — that's not the point. So I got carried away a couple of nights later when me and Simon were babysitting for his mum and dad. We got the cushions off the settee and laid them on the floor and did it there and then, without even turning the telly off. It was 'Stars in their Eyes'. It hurt both of us. I was lying there underneath going, 'Ow, ow,' and he was on top of me going, 'Ow, ow.' It was dead quick. He came, and then it was all over and there we were lying on the floor holding one another. I thought, 'There.' Like, that's that, then.

Then I felt crushed and he got off me. He stood up over me, and I had this view of him above me, past his knob to his face sort of leering down at me, and that's when I went. My spirits just plunged through the floor, and I turned over and stared at the carpet.

'What's the matter? Have I upset you?' asked Simon in a high, surprised voice, but I couldn't say because I didn't know.

'I'm not surprised,' said Annie when we were swopping stories a few days later. 'Doing it with Simon must be like having sex with Mr Nobody. He doesn't seem to want anything, from what you've told me. I've made sure I know exactly what Toby wants.'

I was cross – she was just jealous because I got in first after all. Toby is a baboon. He's got an overhanging forehead. Really – it looks as though he's coming out of a cave all the time. One thing though – it convinced me never to make any more plans, ever again. I was just going to let things happen to me. What was the point? I'd planned and planned and planned this one and I still hadn't got it right, according to Miss Organisation herself, Annie

Turner. I'm just not the sort of person plans work for.

'What does Toby want, then?' I asked her, but she blushed red and wouldn't say. I thought it must be something really kinky, but when she did tell me later, all it was, was for her to wrap her legs around his waist and squeeze hard while they were at it.

'Did you?' I asked.

'No,' she said.

Later on, me and Simon were sitting next to each other on the settee and I'd had a chance to think about it. 'On the floor in front of the telly,' I said, feeling like dirt. '"Stars in their Eyes",' I said.

'Tonight, Matthew, I'm going to be a bit of a goer,' he said and he fell around laughing. Which made me feel a lot better, actually, even though I hit him for saying it.

'I think it was very romantic,' he said, but then he remembered what I thought of romance, and he said, 'Very sexy, I mean.' He held me and kissed me and I soon felt better. The annoying thing was that he was right — it did feel like I'd lost something and he'd got something. But he was also right that it was quite sexy. I never minded sex on the floor on cushions after that, and I never cared about the telly being on. Once we'd done it once, Simon came into his own, I'll give him that. He knew exactly what he wanted. I used to drive him mad with lust. He used to bend and twist my legs all over the place. He used to say he could spend hours just looking at me when I was naked, but it wasn't true — the looking bit usually only lasted about two seconds. I remember lying there with my legs wide open and he was kneeling in between them, having a good look. Then he leaned forward and tickled me down there.

'What's this?' he teased.

'That's my tuppence,' I said.

'More like about thirty thousand million quid,' he told me, and he was on me like a randy old dog.

I went out for nearly two years with Simon and he made me happy, happier than any of the other boys I knew. He loved me, he was in pieces when I stopped seeing him. And you know what? I was in pieces, too. I loved him. I truly did love him, it broke my heart when we split up. Maybe I should have married him and lived with him my whole life and never needed anyone else, but I wasn't ready for that. I wanted to sleep with those rough boys and hang out with those rough girls. He just didn't fit in. So he had to go – Bingo! He went.

When I lost my virginity the second time among the gravestones on the edge of the Southern Cemetery, it was all so different. There was the sound of cars nearby, the wind was blowing all around us, people were watching and I didn't give a toss. Why should I care who watched? Life is so much simpler when you're a dog. All I knew was, I wanted to do it so much it hurt. And then it was just so glorious, so lovely. People say sex for animals isn't as good, but they don't know nothing. The only thing is, I lost interest so quickly you wouldn't believe it. I gave a great big sigh and then I got this scent . . .

'Is this a rabbit?' I snuffed, and began running off to follow it up.

'OW OW OW! Stay still! Stay still!' Poor old Fella! He was stuck in there. He was right up against me, glued tight, running after me as fast as he could with only two legs to go on, gripping tight with his paws round my neck for dear life. He made me think of Simon when we'd done it doggy fashion. I looked over my shoulder at him.

'Aren't you done yet?' I asked. I was!

'I'm not done till you let go.'

'I'm not holding on.'

I decided he was arsing about, so I shot forward to get him out. He howled – OWWWWWW! – fell sideways and slid off me. I felt a sharp twang in my insides and went, 'Ung!' in surprise.

I looked behind me and we were bum to bum. Poor Fella was looking backwards at me, and you should have seen the look on his face. I went, Huf huf huf, he looked so funny. That must hurt!

'Kama Sutra! What a lover!' I said. Then I caught another whiff of rabbit and took a few steps, and of course he had to hobble backwards after me, his dick bent in half.

'Ah! Ah! Ah!' he yelped. 'Lady, stay still! Stay still, Lady!' I took one look and just cracked up. It was so funny! I was laughing so much my legs gave way. Fella gave a great tug and pulled out.

'Ha ha ha!' I howled. 'That was so funny. Your face.

OW OW OW!'

'That'll teach you.' He shook himself from head to toe and grinned at me. 'It was worth it, baby,' he growled. He came over and licked me up, and I licked him back. He was some gorgeous, lovely dog. Good old Fella – always on my side.

'You old dog,' I told him.

'You pretty, pretty little bitch.' We kissed each other, but then, just like last time my spirits just fell out of me and I lay suddenly down in the grass, my nose between my paws.

'What?' asked Fella, licking my nose.

'Is that it?' I asked. 'Is that what dogs do? A minute and that's it?' I felt devastated! I had in my mind those sessions I used to have. We used to roll about the bed for hours. It used to be a night out and now it was just – less than a minute. I mean!

'Right – don't worry. Each time is only quick, but it goes on and on and on for days.'

I felt better after that. Mitch came up, and Fella let him sniff briefly round me. Then we moved off into the older part of the graveyard, hunting for rabbits and mice and voles until the urge took us again. And what a great day that was – the best day of my life! Hunting, playing, chasing, shagging. Fella was right, it was just one thick, misty soup of hormones and sex. Mitch was hanging around as close as he dared to me, just waiting for a chance to slip in, and Fella had to keep chasing him away. I kept giving him the nose so he knew all he had

to do was get me on my own and he was in. It was
funny watching him! He kept finding scents and running
off with Fella, who forgot everything when he was on a
scent. They'd go haring off after it and Mitch would
double back to try and get on me before Fella cottoned
on. He did it too, a couple of times. Fella came back,
sniffed me and sighed, but he didn't do anything about
it. Fair game. It was about ten of Fella to two of Mitch.
Not bad odds, I guess.

If you gotta be a dog, be a bitch. It was just so great,
trotting around town with those two lovely old dogs
panting along behind me. Where I went, they went.
They'd have dropped anything to be by my side.

After a bit, in a sort of half-puzzled way, I found
myself thinking about poor old Terry, left on his tod for
the day. It made me huf, huf to think about him rolling
around on his back in that alley where we left him. He'd
be cross! Gradually, I made my way back, with Fella and
Mitch after me. I was still in a daze – almost got my
brains knocked out on the Princess Parkway. I found his
scent easily enough. I was only half bothered. Did it
with Fella a couple of times under an overgrown apple
tree and then headed out of the alley and into the road
after him.

Terry's is the easiest scent in the world to follow. Pee
and beer and sweat, and a selection of weirdo hormones
– you could sniff him out across a road of busy traffic. I
followed him as far as the swimming pool, and guess

what? He'd disappeared – pop! – just disappeared into thin air. There was his scent by the roadside, and then it stopped. I snuffled bemusedly around for a few minutes while the other two yawned and scratched.

'He's gone,' I said.

'Great,' said Fella.

'He'll be back,' said Mitch.

There was a pause.

'We need to eat,' said Mitch.

'The pack runs tonight,' barked Fella. 'But let's check out the bins behind the shops first.' So we loped off to find scraps. And – I didn't care! My master had gone, and I didn't care. He'd treated me well enough and I'd almost convinced myself that I loved him. But – begging for sausages on the end of a piece of string? What sort of a life was that? The pack – now that was worth living!

You know what? I haven't lived long, but I've packed a lot in. I've known a lot of people and I've done a lot of things, but those days out on the street with the guys, they were the best. Dogs – what a crowd! I'd got bored with Annie and Simon, who were both nice, decent, thoughtful people. I'd been browned off with about five or six different groups of people in the past year. I'd picked them up and dropped them one after the other. I was already getting bored with Michelle and her crowd, even though I'd only been hanging about with them for a few weeks. But I could have hung around with Fella and Mitch forever.

OK, my life could have ended at any second under the wheels of a car, or I might have fallen to the police or any one of the half a billion busy-noses who love to grab a stray by her collar and slap her in the dogs' home, waiting for the needle. But life at the edge tastes so sweet! It's steal or starve, life or death. There's so much more to pack in. The smell of meat – when I walk past a butcher's shop it makes me whine with pleasure to this day. Dog shit and hot fur, spit, grass and breath! Glorious days! My pads sore, my tongue out in the cool air; the dew on my coat, the pack around me and Fella on my back. Boy, we had some fun! And, boy, were we in love with each other. I could talk about it forever, but what for? You can't even imagine the flavour of the things I did.

A dog is a thing no one can imagine. She does what she can without a care and doesn't bother who thinks what about it. She doesn't count her pleasures good or bad – there's just the touch, the scent and the sound. She has her nose to the ground; she can live her life with her eyes shut. Under the moon, she's no one's slave. If her life ends tonight, no one misses her for long but while she's with us, she loves and is loved with passion. She eats until she's full, shits where she likes and communicates with her kind at both ends. With her ears up, her eyes wide and her nose tasting the wide world near and far, past and present, she's hers and her pack's alone. Above all, she is always on the look out for prey. Oh, yes! The dog is a hunting animal – never doubt it!

You have no idea! Heading off a rabbit as he makes his way to the brambles. Cornering a rat in the open road. Yes! The flush of blood and breath that fills the space between your teeth as you crush some little life away. Who can describe the intimacy of a life ending inside your mouth? Once, there was a deer, a huge beast who ran like the wild thing she was. Perhaps she understood that we could think – she screamed for mercy as we closed in. She must have come to graze along the railway line, or escaped from a park, who knows? But she found her way into the city where the pack ran, and that was the end of her.

The pack went up and down in size. The dog-dogs would turn up, mutts who'd slipped the leash or escaped from home to spend a few hours roaming the bins and the gardens and allotments with us. Mitch was there mostly, hunting rabbits, mice and voles in the parks or playing fields, or in the Southern Cemetery. But always, always, always it was me and Fella. I don't think we spent more than a few minutes apart the whole time. We lived to hunt and we hunted to live. We were soul mates, we two, more dog than the dogs themselves, who'd forgotten what it was like to be true to your own nature.

Mitch was a good friend and pack mate, but he was only really ever half there. He was bit dog, bit man, bit nothing. He spent half his evenings moping around the house on Victoria Road where his family still lived, lying behind the hedge in the garden, 'watching over them', as he put it. Watching for what? He liked to think he was still doing them some service, guarding them or something, but no one ever wanted to hurt them.

He loved to watch his children making their way to school, he did it almost every day. As soon as they were out of sight of the house he'd run up to them and let them pat his head and stroke him like he was their pet. 'Half-Dog', Fella called him, and he was right. What did we want with human beings? As the days and nights tumbled past, my life as a person began to seem like a dream to me, one of those anxious dreams that come to you early in the morning as you lie half awake, half asleep, turning over your worries in your mind. The people I knew became distant memories. Sometimes I saw someone I recognised, but although it was only a few weeks ago, it felt far away. I had no desire to follow them up and remind myself.

I felt the past, even my recent doggy past, falling away from me. It was like a terrible weight that had been bound with iron to my neck had suddenly broken and fallen away. To be freed from the past – can you imagine it? It was like growing wings. By the end of another week, I had no idea that I had ever been a human girl called Sandra Francy. All the people that I had once known and loved and hated evaporated out of my mind. If I saw my mum on the street during that time, I don't think I'd have even recognised her. A dog lives by her nose, her wits, and her eyes and her ears. What use is memory to us? Poor Mitch was crippled by his humanity. Perhaps that was why he was unable to enjoy that most perfect of pleasures, the sweetest bone in the whole carcass – cats!

Late at night when the people have gone to their beds, the cats come out. They think the night belongs to them. The garbage bins, the gardens and roads, the spaces under the cars – it's their territory; so they think. People don't bother cats, and what cat ever got caught by a dog? But they hadn't met us before. We're something different.

We tried everything, me and Fella! We spent whole nights discussing tactics and tricks. We called to them, we shouted at them, we barked at them. One of us hid round a corner in ambush, while the other chased cats towards them. We went down drains, on roofs, we hid in alleyways and shrubberies, on the tops of cars and behind hedges. We hid in bins in Chinatown for hours, waiting for the lanky brindled tom who sprayed there at the same time every night. We even broke into houses in an effort to trap them in their own homes, but we never caught one. Fella had this one trick he was certain was going to work. We must have tried it about six hundred times, an ancient plan of his to catch a cat on its own territory – up in a tree.

'Imagine the terror of the cat! Imagine the joy of the dog!' he barked enthusiastically, rolling his eyes and wagging his tail so hard that his whole bum banged from side to side.

It worked like this. We'd find a small tree, something with branches fairly low to the ground, out in the open

– we wanted to be sure the cat would make for it when the chase began. Then came the hard bit – getting Fella up into the branches. Sometimes he'd do it in stages – onto a wheelie-bin, then a window ledge, then a garage roof, then into the tree. Other times, if we could get Mitch to join in, we'd do it by forming a tower of dogs – me on the ground, Mitch on my back and then Fella would have to clamber up on top of us and reach the branches that way.

Next thing was to wait for a cat to get near enough to the tree to go up it when we chased it. Fella, precariously balanced up there, would be peering out trying to spot one, trying to keep his trap shut. Quite often he'd fall out several times before we finally got it sorted and we'd have to start all over again. The plan was, once the cat was treed, it would relax. It would probably even turn round and look at us on the ground, hissing and taunting us. Then, Fella would suddenly and silently seize it in his jaws and bite the life out of it.

That was the theory; but Fella could never contain himself. All he had to do was wait, then drop quietly onto the cat, or at least push it down into my waiting jaws. But he never could. As soon as pussy was two leaps up the trunk, a fusillade of ferocious barking and abuse would emerge, not from the ground, but from the quivering tree itself. The poor cat would cling on for a second, frozen in surprise and terror. Every hair on its body would stand on end. It would open its jaws and wait for a split second for its hearing to come to its senses and make the barking come from a sensible place. Then, it would catch Fella's scent up there with it. With a great yowl, the cat would leap into the air and come down, claws flailing – just as I rushed up! But we never caught one. They were so full of terror they always shot off like rockets, once or twice even running over my actual teeth. Fella would fall out of the tree snarling with excitement and rage and we'd have an argument.

'You shoulda caught it, you shoulda caught it, you shoulda caught it!' he barked.

'You shoulda waited, you shoulda waited, you shoulda waited!' I barked back.

'You shoulda caught it! You shoulda caught it! It fell into your mouth!'

'You barked! You barked!' I told him. 'If you didn't bark you'd be able to sneak up and get them.'

'I'm a dog,' he growled. 'Dogs don't sneak.'

'Dogs don't climb trees, either,' I pointed out.

'You try it then,' he snarled. So I did, but he was right. It was impossible not to bark when you got that near a cat. Even a dog that was once human can't do it.

Mitch sometimes joined in cat hunts, but afterwards he was always full of undoglike shame and guilt. He'd creep back after the chase on his belly, licking his lips and whining miserably. He swore it was beneath us, that it was disgusting, unhygienic – anything he could think of. So he said – but when the little pussies ran he was off after them, his feet helpless beneath him, and his disgust never returned until they'd got away.

'It's like some horrible addiction,' he groaned. But he was utterly unable to help himself.

It was a cat that gave us one of our most bizarre nights of fun. It happened like this: Fella knew a house where we were certain to get a cat. He didn't say how he knew of this house, but he swore that a cat slept on the hearthrug every night in a locked room, and that the window was left open for it to get in and out. It sounded too good to be true.

Well, we got there. There was the garden, just as he had said, there was the window and when we peered in, there was the dark little mound of the cat, curled up and fast asleep.

Without another word, Fella jumped up and dived straight in the window, for once in his life in total silence. Taken by surprise, I stood and watched through the glass. He hit the floor with a thud and raced straight over to the cat. Puss woke up at the thud of him landing and spent a vital second watching, thinking perhaps that it was a nightmare streaking across the carpet towards her. Then, like a rocket-powered furball the terrified animal leaped up, tried to climb the air, failed – and fell directly onto Fella's head. She jumped off and in two bounds was half way up the curtains. But, ha! As puss was looking down at Fella, who was growling like a demon, I got my head in the window. Hearing the clash of my teeth, the miserable creature looked up to see my slavering, foaming jaws and wild staring eyes climbing down towards her. Luckily for puss I got stuck half in, half out of the window. By the time I'd wriggled through and fell, barking and snapping onto my mouth on the carpet, she and Fella were out of the lounge door, which was open after all, and off into the house.

I ran after them, up the stairs and into a bedroom at the front. Fella jumped up onto the bed, I followed him and the man and woman sleeping there awoke to the sound of us bursting into a terrible fit of barking. How they screamed! They both leapt to their feet and tried to clamber up the wall, screaming and shrieking. Then, in amongst all the racket someone said, 'Shut up, you fool, the cat'll get away!' in a clear, deep voice.

I started and looked around. It was human speech — who else was in the room with us? Then the voice cried out, 'It's me, sweetheart. Look at me! Look at me!'

It was Fella. Suddenly he could speak! But where did he get his voice from? For a moment I was terrified, but he found the whole thing hilarious. Coughing with laughter, he fell off the bed and rolled about on the rug.

'Ha ha ha!' he yelled. 'Ha hahahaha!'

'Omigod, it's talking, it's talking again. Itscomebackforme! Aahhhahhhhhh!' said the woman. 'Keepitaway- ah!- helpmehelpmehelpme! Aahhhh!' Fella clashed his jaws, lolled out his tongue, rolled his eyes, and winked at me.

'Put a sock in it, you'll wake the neighbours', he said, and started laughing again. 'Lady! Baby! Let's goooooo!' he yelled, and galloped off out of the room. Amazed, I jumped off the bed and ran after him. He was laughing so much he fell downstairs, and lay at the bottom, shouting, 'Ha, ha, ha!' in his horrible new human voice. It was infectious; I was giggling myself by this time. We just about made it out of the window and fell onto the lawn where we lay for a while, laughing helplessly.

I was astonished! Fella had often tried to speak human but he'd never been even remotely successful before. Now he jumped up and ran down the street, shouting, 'Fire! Mad Dog!' and 'Help me!' at the top of his voice. You could hear people screaming as he went past.

We spent the next few hours running up and down Didsbury, shouting and barking at people. You should have seen their faces! You should have heard their screams! It was the scariest, best fun I ever had! Later, when Fella got his good old bark back, we realised that we had missed a perfect opportunity to hunt for cats – with that voice we could have called them to us for certain!

'Maybe it was more fun hunting humans,' said Fella, and he stopped to stare madly at me. 'Maybe it's their blood we want to taste,' he hissed. He made me shiver from head to foot, but quite deliciously. You never could tell when Fella was teasing and when he wasn't.

I asked him how it had happened with the voice, and he just shrugged and said he didn't know. But Mitch told me later that he knew that house, and the woman in it, only too well.

'That's his girlfriend, from the old days. He still visits her from time to time. He'd been living with her for almost a year when Terry got him. He was only young, but he loved her. Sometimes –' and Mitch dropped his voice – 'Sometimes, you know, he catches a rabbit and leaves it for them on the back step. If he stayed a little longer he'd see it go into the dustbin. It's all he can do for her. But don't tell him I told you! He doesn't know I know. He thinks he's being weak.'

And you know what? So did I! I had no thoughts at all about the people I once knew, whoever they were. I didn't even want to know. When I asked Fella if that had been his old girlfriend, he admitted it but he swore she meant nothing to him any more, now that he had me. We went back twice to see if he could get the voice again, but the windows were all locked forever after.

SEVEN

How long did I run with the pack? As you forget yourself,
the past falls away behind you like a cliff crumbling at your
heels. Each day I was more and more a dog, more and
more myself. Before long I never even bothered to remember what I had been doing yesterday. Mitch's stubborn
hanging about outside his old human home seemed like an
illness, or some sort of affectation. I could have run forever
if we'd changed our hunting grounds, but one day I saw
someone sitting on the pavement, and my heart moved
inside me. I had no idea if it was going up or down.

'Who's that?'

'I told you he'd come back,' growled Mitch. Fella
started fawning and running up and down, trying to
entice me away but it was already too late. I was walking
forward, my nose in the air, sniffing, testing, recognising.
Then I knew. It was Terry! Terry, Terry, my Terry, who
fed me and slept with me and got sausages for me! With
a joyful bark I bounded forward, hardly hearing the groan
of disappointment from Fella behind me. Terry saw me
and lifted his hands to take me back.

'Lady! You're still here! Oh, you good girl! Oh, you
lovely good girl, have you been waiting all this time for

me? Good girl, Lady!' I crouched and wagged and licked his hands and sniffed in his pocket for a sausage, overcome with happiness.

Terry got a piece of string out of his pocket and tied it around my neck, all the time with his eyes sideways, like a frightened horse, watching every move Fella and Mitch made. Fella just stood there with his lips curled up around his gums, but he didn't do anything. Terry stood up, glanced up and down, and led me away up the road. Fella and Mitch stood and watched, left behind on the pavement. After we had gone a few steps Mitch barked, and when I looked back he was standing there, looking intently at me and wagging his tail. Fella just stood by his side as if he couldn't believe what was happening. I whined, looked up at Terry and pulled briefly back. But Terry tugged the lead.

'Leave, Lady, leave! Come on, girl!' I wagged my tail and followed. He led me round the corner, and as soon as we were out of sight of the dogs, he fell to his knees and patted my sides and my head and stroked my muzzle until I thought I'd faint with pleasure. We went for a walk into the park and round the streets, and when we came back to Copson Street, I barely noticed that Fella and Mitch had gone.

Terry tied me up and went into Somerfield's. I stood staring in through the door the whole time, trying to catch a glimpse of him to make sure he really was in there, he really was going to come out and bring sausages with him. When he caught sight of me down the aisles, he gave me the thumbs-up and winked. Oh, sausages! Sure enough, when he came out his pockets were bulging and he smelt like heaven. I was jumping up and pawing him and licking my lips. Sausages! How could I have forgotten sausages! We went to the bench and he fed them to me, one after the other. They slid down my throat, and my whole body filled up with fat and ground meat and joy. When they were all gone, I sighed like a puppy, and lay down at his feet. It was bliss. All I wanted to do was lie there and listen to his sweet voice murmur away, as my stomach digested my meal.

Terry grinned at me as he downed his beer. 'Well, what do you think, girl?' he said. 'Do I look better for my stay in Her Majesty's? And I don't mean the theatre. They feed you but they don't let you drink.' He lifted his can of Special Brew and waved it in the air, wrinkling his nose. 'I can hardly get the stuff down my neck, but that'll change with a bit of practice.' He winked and laughed and took a swig. 'I suppose the break was good for me,' he went on. 'Ten days in the slammer. Questions. Endless questions! What were you doing, when did you last do this, when did you last do that? The girl, the girl, the girl.' He looked curiously at me and said, 'And which girl was that, Lady? Sandra? Remember her?' I lifted my eyebrows and gazed apathetically at him. It was just one more name in the long list of human beings who no longer meant anything to me. Terry laughed and rubbed my head. He seemed to be feeling very perky. 'It seems there's been a disappearance round here. Nice girl, good home — a bit wild,

148

but . . . Mum didn't approve of her friends. Part of growing up. A phase she was going through!' He laughed again, crossed his legs, put his arm back on the bench. He was happy. People were glancing at him as they went past — the poor drunk, so young and so hopeless already, talking to his dog as she dozed on the pavement.

'Spending too much time out, hanging about on street corners, not doing her homework. And boys! Too many boys. We know the sort, don't we, Lady?' Hearing my name, I barked and wagged my tail. 'Bit of an old slapper. Eh, girl? Bit of a bloody old slapper.' And he laughed again and scratched my ears, and he was just as pleased as anything.

'Did you have a good time running around with the dogs?' he said. 'Some things never change, do they? You liked running off and hanging around on the street then, and you like it now.' He sighed. 'I ought to give you a whipping for leaving me like that — but those ol' hormones, eh, Sandra? You can't beat 'em. Unless you drink enough, of course.' He finished his can and went to buy another. I was puzzled. Why was he calling me Sandra? But Terry often rambled when he was drunk. I didn't care. I'd been away a long time and I was pleased to be back.

After a while we set off out of Withington and made our way along the Wilmslow Road towards the Universities to beg. As we walked, Terry had me practising my words — 'Sausages,' 'Cheers, mate!' and so on. We'd got as far as the outskirts of Rusholme when he stopped in front of a lamp-post and started to chuckle to himself.

'Look at this! Have you seen this? But you're so low to the ground, you poor four-legged beastie. Look!' he was pointing to a piece of paper at the height of a human's head on the lamp-post.

'Who's that, then?' he said in a teasing voice. Then, stooping down, he picked me up bodily and held me so I could see.

It was a picture of a girl. She had long, dark brown hair, and a pretty, plump face. She was amused by something. Her eyes were sideways and she was smiling like she'd just been caught doing something she shouldn't have. As I stared my heart began to sink like a marble in a pool of syrup, I had no idea why. Suddenly I was terrified. Who was this girl, what was she to me that she could collapse my heart like this? Underneath the photo was writing.

Have you seen this girl?

The police are concerned to discover the whereabouts of Sandra Francy who was last seen in the company of an unknown man in Copson Street M14, at about four o'clock in the afternoon on 6th April. She was wearing a brown hooded fleece-type coat and velvet trousers. If you have seen Sandra, or have any knowledge of her whereabouts, please contact the missing persons' help line at this number immediately.

Terry put me down on the floor, took up my lead and walked on as if nothing had happened. I tried to follow, but my legs had turned to slush. I was devastated. I felt as if he had whipped me, I was so full of shame and pain. But why? I didn't even know who that girl was! In my mind's eye there flashed a stream of other people, all of them connected in some way to each other – people I knew and yet didn't know; a woman called Mum, a man called Dad. What did it all mean?

And then, then, oh, Lord, the memories began to crowd back in on me. One after the other, the people I knew and loved and had forgotten so utterly fell back into place in my mind and heart – my poor mum! How long had I been gone? Julie, Adam – I remembered the tears in their eyes that time I'd hidden behind the wall and spied on them. Simon! Why had I hurt him so badly – why had I hurt us both so badly? Why did I have to hurt everyone who ever came near me?

The memories crowded in. I rolled helplessly over onto my back, exposing myself, and began to howl. Terry bent down over me, glancing nervously up and down the street, as if passers-by would think he'd hurt the poor dog.

'Come on, girl, you're attracting attention. Stand up, will you? Lady, please!'

. . . School, my teachers, my friends, Annie – all those people and places that had meant so much to me – gone, from my life, from my mind! I'd lost the value of everything and here I was on the end of a piece of string in the hands of the man who had done it to me! How could I be so stupid? How could I be so *selfish*?

'Will you get up?' groaned Terry. He grabbed my neck and tried to pull me up but I just lay there. There were tears in his eyes. 'I'm sorry, Lady, but we're in it together, don't you see?' he murmured. I thought, In it together? Together? With the man who had robbed me of everything? And in that second I was full of rage. I twisted from under his hand, leapt to my feet and sprang at him. I fully intended to tear out his throat. Terry's hands flew up to protect himself, he fell back with a cry and I was over him, my legs around him, my teeth worrying at his face and at the clothes around his neck. I seized one of his hands and bit; the blood ran. I heard cries around me. Out of the corner of my eye I saw people running. I paused for one last savage mauling at the soft flesh above his wrists, and then I was off, with a speed no human could ever match. But had they been able to see, those people shouting at the savage animal, they would have seen that I was no ordinary dog, for tears were running from my eyes and blinding me as I ran.

I cried all the way home, but when I got there I had no idea what to do. Run up to my mum and sniff her bum? Lick her hands? I was a dog, I didn't even have lips that could kiss. But at last I had something that I never had before: tears. Maybe they were a sign that at last, I was ready to change back and become myself again.

I rushed down Yew Tree Road, skidded to a halt

outside the front garden and sniffed the air outside the house. It was weird, because I knew every scent there but it was all suddenly so alien. All the familiar scents of Mum, Julie, Adam and our household things were just the same, but my dog's nose magnified them a thousand times. I was so disorientated that I staggered up and down in front of the wall, trying not to fall over. It was like seeing familiar people blown up, with huge wobbly heads or giant features swollen out of proportion.

I put my paws on the low wall in front of our house and looked over at that familiar view I'd so nearly forgotten. The front door was slightly open, as if the house was inviting me back. My heart broke. My heart was always breaking these days. How could it ever be fitted together again? I thought, What happens to you when your heart breaks too often, do you go mad? But I must already be mad for this to happen to me. Perhaps all this was a dream and I was asleep all the time, lying in a ward in a mental hospital with my parents hanging over my bed, asking the doctors if there was any improvement, still loving me even though I was barking mad.

I sat back down and wiped the tears out of my eyes with the sides of my paws. My tears comforted me. My misery was human, if nothing else. I had recovered my memory. I was still a human being inside.

In the space of just one hour, my life had been turned upside down all over again. How was it possible that I had forgotten everything? Perhaps it was because I was still turning more and more into a dog – perhaps it was a defence mechanism to make the horror of what had happened more bearable. But now that I'd remembered again who I was and what I'd lost, the life I had been enjoying so much seemed revolting to me. It was pathetic! Living out of dustbins, hanging around on the street, shagging on the road and chasing cats as if I was worth nothing. And the joy I'd felt when I found Terry again — what for? So I could sit around on the end of a piece of string, begging to keep him in drink? Wagging my tail like a slut for a few free sausages? Why did I treat myself like that? I had to go home. I had to put myself at the mercy of my family. Somehow, I had to make them understand that however hairy I was on the outside, inside I was still their loving daughter. In the past, when I'd caused them so much worry with my wild ways, they were always ready to forgive me and take me back on any terms. Love is the strongest thing on this earth — I truly believe that to be so. Love can see through to our hearts. I still shared that with my mum and dad, and with Adam and Julie!

I jumped over the wall and ran up to the door.

I knew where everyone was. My nose told me. Mum was in the kitchen. Adam and Julie weren't there, but someone else was. It took me a moment to recognise it, because my new senses made everything as if I was looking into a twisted mirror. My dad! He must have come home, all the way from America. Just for a second my heart sank. Why had he come back to live at home as soon as I'd gone? Had he hated me so much he couldn't bear to live with me?

But then I shook my head. Of course not, he'd come back out of love – he loved me and wanted me home. Well, I was home. I told myself to stop telling me lies, nosed the door aside and ran quickly upstairs to my room. It was closed, but I managed to open it by grabbing the handle with my jaws, pulling down and pushing with my hind legs on the floor. Once inside, I pushed it shut and drew the bolt to with my teeth. That was hard, it made my mouth bleed. But I was home – back in my own room. With a whimper of relief, I flung myself onto my bed and wept, and wept and wept until the fur on my face was sodden.

But I didn't have much time to spare for tears. Pretty soon I heard my dad coming up the stairs to use the toilet. On the way back he paused outside my room and I held my breath – it was too soon, I wasn't ready! But he sighed and walked past. Sooner or later someone would discover that my door was locked – from the inside. If only they knew how much their missing daughter wanted them to come in, but of course I couldn't allow that to happen – not yet.

A little later, the front door opened and Adam came in. He called hello to Mum and Dad, and straightaway asked if they'd heard anything.

'Nothing,' said Mum in a dead, flat voice. I wondered if Dad was putting his arm around her shoulder like he used to in the old days. Then, the old guilts came flooding back again like a flock of birds. Maybe now that I was gone, they'd get back together. Maybe it was me

155

who had driven them apart. Maybe Adam was asking if I'd been found in the hope that they'd found my dead body . . .

'Stop torturing yourself,' I growled to myself. Things were bad enough – why make it *worse*? As if everything was going to be all right for everyone else just because I wasn't there! As if I was that important! I made up my mind, even though I was just a dog, that from then on I was going to behave in a grown-up manner and do whatever I could to make the best of things. What was the point of feeling sorry for myself? I had to learn to cope with things the way they were.

What could I do to show them who I was? They wouldn't be able to recognise my voice, but maybe my handwriting would be all right. Why not? I jumped up to try it straightaway, but of course I couldn't even open the drawer to get at my pens and crayons. I found a lipstick on the desk, so I tried that, wedging it between my toes, but of course it didn't work. I simply didn't have the muscles. I tried to hold it in my mouth – that was better, but the results were still disappointing. My handwriting was worse than ever.

I realised that I could never tell them who I was: I'd have to show them. The thing was, I told myself, *to refuse to behave like a dog*. If I was going to be human, I had to behave like a human being. I had to *be* Sandra Francy.

Up till now I'd just given in. I'd been behaving like a dog – how did I expect to change? Well, from now on I vowed that I was going to do nothing that dogs do. No more cats, no more eating off the ground, no more hunting. No more peeing and crapping in public, I was going to use the toilet. No more going naked; I would wear clothes. No more barking and growling – I was going to use human speech even if I made a complete fool of myself. I'd brush my teeth, wash my hair and clip my toe nails. I'd watch TV and read books. I'd even start my studies again – my school books were all here in my room. I could still learn, even though I was a dog. I was going to do everything the way people do it. Terry couldn't make me human, neither could my parents. I had to do it myself.

Looking back, it seems naïve of me to think that being human was just about how you eat your dinner, or how often you brush your teeth, or what clothes and make-up you wear. Being human is more than that. It's about responsibility, about caring for people, about priorities, about respecting yourself. All that stuff. But it was a start. Maybe just the act of trying so hard to convince people of what I was like inside was something human in itself.

I jumped down off the desk and ran to my chest of drawers. It was a new one, fortunately, with the drawers on runners, so they were quite easy to open. There inside were all my clothes, although how I was ever going to get them on I didn't know. I dug about with my mouth and dumped them on the carpet – my tee-shirts, my knickers, my tights, my jeans and skirts and tops. Then, for the first time in weeks, I got dressed.

I found my nice little tee-shirt, the one with the yellow

and blue stripes. I did that first, holding the sides with my paws and pushing my head in. It used to be as tight as skin but now, of course, it was all baggy, and I thought, At least I'm losing weight! And I went huf, huf, huf. Laughing made me feel better. I thought, Wow, look at me, I haven't lost my sense of humour. I was almost having a good time!

The tee-shirt was hard enough, but the knickers were horrendous. I had to spread them out on the floor, stand in the leg holes and then pull them up with my teeth. It reminded me of some horrible bloke at school teasing me by saying that I'd had my knickers off for so long, I'd forgotten how to put them on. He didn't know how right he was! It took me ages, but I did it. Then I tried to do the same with my tights, but that was just too hard. I had to keep doing little jumps to get my feet off them, while pulling them up with my teeth at the same time. It was impossible – but I didn't let myself get discouraged. I thought, One step at a time. Knickers today, tights tomorrow.

Next, I tried to put some bottoms on. My jeans and trousers were all too long, so in the end I settled for a short black skirt I often used to wear with that top. Then I climbed back up onto the table – it was hard in all that clobber – and had a look at myself. I nearly wept. I used to be so pretty and sexy in that little skirt and that tight top. Now, I just looked ridiculous.

I tried some make-up. Holding the lipstick down between my paws, I rubbed my black dog lips around the red stick, but it was such a hopeless mess, I licked it all off and tried again. I got better, but after several goes, I decided that make-up with a hairy face and no fingers is definitely a no-go – but I did feel that my paw skills were already getting better. I jammed the lippy between my toes and, holding myself up with one paw on the mirror, I had another go at writing. Then I jumped back onto the bed to have a look.

'I am home,' it said, in great ugly letters. It was just about legible. I was as proud as if I'd written a work of art.

And then – well! – it was now or never. Time to introduce myself to my family.

I opened the bolt with my teeth, then spent minutes over the difficult job of opening the door and pulling it towards me at the same time. At last, with blood in my mouth, I stepped out onto the landing. Downstairs I could hear the murmur of voices from the sitting room. They were watching TV, all together without me. I thought, How could they! But then I remembered my resolution to grow up. What did I expect them to do, spend every minute of the day weeping over me? Give up everything nice because I wasn't there? Life goes on, Sandra, I told myself, with you or without you. It's up to you to make sure you're there to join in.

I was determined to get down those stairs on two legs. I got up, balancing delicately and tried to put a foot down the first step but it was too high for my little leggies. I tried to hop down – and, disaster! I fell. I reached out with my front legs, but they got tangled in the tee-shirt, and I bumped and rolled all the way down to the bottom. Ouch! What a start to my first day back as a real girl!

Inside the lounge I could hear my mum saying, 'What's that?' I jumped up quickly – I had to get into the room before they got out to see what was going on. Luckily for me, the latch to the sitting room door never quite catches, so I was able to push it open with my nose. Then, I stood up on my hind legs and walked in to greet my family.

My mother was the first to begin screaming, followed closely by Adam and Dad, both of them bellowing like gorillas. They all leaped out of their chairs and backed into the wall. Dad had to leap right over the sofa to get back there with the others. The noise was so bad I fell forward onto all fours in fright, which made them howl all over again. Maybe they thought I was going for them.

As I struggled to get upright, my mother was yelling, 'Mad dog! Mad dog!' at the top of her voice. Adam, great, big, hairy, strong Adam, was trying to hide behind her. He was going, 'Keep it away from me! Keep it away from me!' in his loud, booming voice. My dad was standing in front of them with his arms spread out protectively as if I was going to try and get past him to savage them.

'My God, what is it?'

'It's wearing her clothes! Oh my God! It's wearing her clothes!' howled my mother.

'Ssssh! You'll scare it,' hissed my dad, and both Mum and Adam stopped howling in the same second. There was a terrified pause in which I made it back onto my hind feet and smiled at them. They all hissed in fear and backed off into the corner. It was lucky I was between them and the door, or they'd have been out and away.

'It's the same one I was telling you about,' said my mum, in a terrified whisper. 'The one that came here.' She paused and then added in a horrified tone, 'It was the same day she disappeared.'

'Why's it got her clothes on? What's going on?' demanded Adam tearfully.

It was time to say something. I knew from practising that 'd's were hard; so were 'm's at the beginning of words but they were easier if they were in the middle, so I tried with my brother first. I looked at him and I said,

'Adam. Adam. Help.'

It came out beautifully. Perfect! The word just fell out of my lips as clear as a bell. 'Help' was a bit of a mess, I admit – it sounded more like 'Hrwworwwap.' But still – not bad for a dog.

'It knows my name,' said Adam, and he fainted. Almost fainted, anyway. His knees sort of gave way and he fell to the ground. My dad caught him by the elbow and steadied him. Suddenly he was about three feet tall, like a dwarf between Mum and Dad. 'Ha, ha! Ha!' I went. I couldn't help being a bit pleased. That would get him back for all the times he hid behind the door and made grunting noises to scare me.

Mum put her hands to her mouth. 'Oh my God,' she whispered. 'What's happening? What sort of an animal is it?'

I said, 'Mum,' but it didn't sound anything like. I tried Dad. It came out like a little bark, but it wasn't bad. 'Droow, drogghw, droughwd. Hrwworp,' I said.

'What's it saying now?' he asked suspiciously.

'It called you Dad,' said Adam.

My mother groaned. 'It's some sort of evil trick! Someone must have kidnapped her and they've trained this horrible dog to wear her clothes and speak as if it knows us.' She stared at me wildly and then suddenly screamed, 'I can't take any more!' and she fell to her knees, screaming and weeping and hacking at the air with her hands. I felt terrible – I didn't want to do this to her. But what else could I do?

Then Adam said, 'Its knickers have fallen down.'

I looked down – it was true! They were around my ankles. As I looked the skirt went down after it. They could see everything! I blushed bright red under my fur and dropped to all fours to hide myself, and the whole family immediately started screaming like maniacs. I turned round to grab the knickers and pull them up, and while my eyes were hidden, Adam made a run for the door. I had to jump dead quick and snap my teeth in order to herd him back into the room. After that there was a terrible, bizarre minute as they started screaming and running from one side of the room to the other, half trying to get out of my way, half trying to get past me,

162

while I was trying to stand up and grab my knickers in my teeth and pull them up, while at the same time keeping them away from the door and trying to dodge my dad, who kept swinging kicks at me every time I looked away. It was just about impossible. Then I thought, What am I worrying about the knickers for? OK, I didn't want any of them to see my hairy bits, but since I was hairy all over, what did it matter?

I thought, Sod it, I'm going too fast. I needed to show them I was friendly.

So I did the tricks, the dog tricks. You know the ones. You've seen them a hundred times before. I sat back on my bum, put my paws up under my chin, wagged my tail and whined. I waved one of my paws. It's called begging.

There was a pause. 'She wants to be friends,' said my dad.

'Just get rid of it!' shrieked Mum. But she was peeping through her fingers at me. I rolled onto my back and waved my paws in the air, trying to look cute. Me, cute! Anyone who knows me would stare at you in amazement if you told them I wanted to look cute. In fact, it was just embarrassing, rolling about with no knickers in front of them all, but what else could I do? Dad smiled and held out his hand. 'Good girl! Good girl!' he said. I wagged my tail and lopped my tongue out.

'Be careful, she could turn again any minute,' said Mum.

'There's a good girl!' said Dad. He stepped gradually

forward. I just lay there. At last he was close enough to bend down and tickle my tummy. I could have wept with gratitude.

'She's a good dog, not savage at all. You're not savage, are you?' he asked me hopefully. I whined and wagged my tail bravely and licked his hand while he made friends. Then he stood up. I followed him. He pushed me gently to one side, and gave Adam and Mum a nod at the door. They eased their way past me, out of the door. Then Dad jumped out after them and slammed the door behind him.

'Call the police,' my mum yelled. 'Call the police and get the bloody thing put down!'

The whole room shuddered around the slammed door. I was stunned. The first chance to get away from me and they'd taken it. They hadn't given me a chance! But – what was the point? I didn't blame them, how could I? I was a dog! In fact, I wasn't even that. I was neither one thing nor the other. I was just a useless, stupid bitch, who couldn't talk properly, couldn't bark properly, couldn't do anything properly.

So this was it. Police, the cells, the dogs' home and then put down, unless some kind family adopted me. But who was I kidding? Who was going to want a weirdo dog like me? I lay down on the floor, put my paws over my nose, and waited for the end to come.

But my life wasn't over yet – and help came from just where I least expected it. After about five minutes the door opened – just the slightest crack. I cocked an

164

eye and saw my mum's face peering in at me. I raised my eyebrows, wagged my tail slowly, but I didn't move. I wanted to look slow. I wanted to look friendly. I wanted to look safe.

The door opened a little more, wider . . . wider. She moved into the room. I dared to lift my head, still wagging my tail slowly so she knew I meant her no harm. She came in another step. Now she was standing a few feet in, with the door open behind her.

'Don't you come near me!' she whispered. I didn't move. She licked her lips and glanced around the room. I've never seen her look so pale.

'Who would do such a thing?' she whispered, as if she didn't want anyone to know she was in there. 'My Sandra's clothes!'

I slowly got to my feet, and Mum let out a little silent scream, so I backed off. I sat down and begged.

'Silly tricks,' she scoffed. She was holding her chest as if her heart might stop with fright. She glanced behind her, out of the open door. I had the idea that Dad and Adam didn't know she was in there with me. 'Who taught you about us?' she said. 'Oh, if only you could really talk!'

I thought of trying to say something, but nothing seemed to scare my family as much as my voice. Instead, I stood on my hind legs like a person, but she didn't like that either.

'Stop it,' she snapped. 'Stand like a dog.'

Obediently I went on all fours. Mum's hand was at her

mouth again, her finger inside for a nail to chew like she always did when she was anxious. Her nails were always half way down her fingers. 'As if you could understand a single word!' she said. I nodded my head to show that I understood everything, and she closed her eyes and shook her head violently. But she must have trusted me a little more, because she came closer. Gradually she got right up to me. I whined and she laughed.

'You seem friendly enough, anyway,' she said. Then she did a curious thing; she went to the door and closed it. Then she stood there chewing on the skin on the edge of her finger.

'This is girls' talk, isn't it, just you and me,' she said, with a sickly smile. 'Gareth's gone up with Adam to his room so we have a few minutes before the police arrive. Why not?'

She looked sharply at me and said, 'Sit,' and I sat. 'Stand,' she said, and I stood. 'Get up on the sofa,' she said, and I did. 'Turn round. Lie down.' I did all her commands, and then came the true tests. 'Count to three, pat your paw on the carpet,' she said. Joyfully I patted the carpet three times. Now I knew she half believed that I was not just a dog. 'Three times four?' she asked. I did twelve. 'Seven minus six?' I did one.

'Oh my God. Oh my God,' she said. She walked twice around the room. I just sat and watched. It was all in her hands, everything was in her hands. My future. My life. Then she said, 'What's eight sevens?' I just stared at her – what on earth was it? She had to do hard ones! I racked my brains and began tapping out, trying to buy time, but she interrupted me by laughing.

'Now, if you knew the answer to that, then I'd know you're not my Sandra. Sevens were never a strong point, were they?' But then she scowled again because she'd admitted what was on her mind. She started chewing her finger again and wandered around the room some more.

'It's not possible, of course it's not, no matter how clever you are. Just not possible! The only thing is — how come you're wearing the top that she always wore with that skirt? Who knew that? And how come -' and her voice shrank down to a whisper — 'how come you've got the top on back to front? Because my Sandra, she always wore it back to front. We used to have arguments about it. She liked the low back at the front because she wanted to show a bit of cleavage, and I tried to stop her but I never managed it. Now, how on earth could you know that? How could anyone know that?'

My heart was soaring inside me! I whined and pawed the ground and nodded my head. I wanted to be able to hug her and tell her everything! I opened my jaws and I said, 'Mum!' But she put her hands over her ears.

'Don't talk!' she said. 'Answer me this instead. Listen. Listen. Me and my Sandra. Listen. Do you remember when you needed your first bra? We were all out on a shopping trip, the whole family, me, you, Julie and Adam. Do you remember? You were furious. You thought we should go into town, just you and me. A girls' trip. You sulked all day. I thought you were being horrible, but when I realised what it was I was so sorry. So the next week I took you in on your own and bought you some clothes. Just you and me. Remember?'

Yes, of course I remembered. I'd been really angry about that business with the bra, even though I knew she'd tried to make it up to me.

'All right,' she said. 'What did I get you?'

Yes! Yes! My brown and gold top! How could I forget? I loved that top, I wore it and wore it. It'd been my favourite thing for years. I barked excitedly and nodded my head – yes yes . . . yes yes . . . yes yes!

With a flourish Mum opened the door. 'Go on then, smart-arse. Fetch!' she commanded.

Oh, my clever, clever mum! With a bark of joy I bounded out of the door and up the stairs. My door was shut. I scratched and whined and jumped up for the handle, and then of course Adam's opened, slammed immediately and Dad shouted from behind it, 'It's out! Look out, Sue, it's out!'

But Mum called, 'I let her out. Leave her!'

'You let her out? What for? For God's sake!'

Then I got the door open and with a joyous woof, I ran into the bedroom and began nosing around in the heap of clothes on the floor. There it was, the lovely old thing, worn to bits and far too small now, but I still loved it with its velvet stripes and pretty, pale metallic strips in between. I ran downstairs and I dropped it at my mother's feet and looked up to her and . . . and . . .

There was a long silence. My dad was standing on the

168

stairs behind us. My nose told me Adam was behind him. My mum looked down at me and . . .

'Oh, Sandra! Oh, my darling, darling darling – Oh, Sandra, what's happened to you? What have they done?'

She bent and scooped me up with her arms, and held me tightly to her, kissing me and loving me and weeping tears. And I was weeping tears too, flooding down my face. I just wanted to cry and to show her how I could cry, as if tears alone would wash me back to what I was.

My mum! What about her? Can you believe it? How many people could pick their daughter out of a horrible hairy face full of fangs and a tongue like a face flannel? Could your mum do that for you? 'Cause my mum did it for me!

'For heaven's sake, Susan!' cried my father at the door, and his face was a twisted mask of despair at seeing his wife – his ex-wife, anyway – holding on to a little bitch dog and claiming it was her daughter.

'It's her! Do you think I don't know my own child, just because she looks like a dog?' demanded Mum furiously. Dad took a couple of paces towards her, but she turned her back on him. 'How else could she know all those things? It's her! Only she's – she's been turned into something else . . . '

'What are you saying?' began Dad, but he was interrupted by a knock at the door.

'The police!' wailed Mum. 'Get rid of them, get rid of them, and we'll talk then. Don't say a word, just get rid of them!' She ran up the stairs, pushing past him.

Adam dodged back out of our way, and she ran along the landing to her room.

'Just get rid of them!' she rasped. She dived into her bedroom and slammed the door.

'Sandra! My darling, oh, my darling,' she cried. She put me down on the bed, threw herself down next to me and covered my wet nose with her kisses and let me lick the tears from her poor, tired old face.

To tell you the truth, it's not the first time Mum's had to hustle me up the stairs with the police banging on the door, looking for me. In fact, it was only a few weeks ago that it happened the first time, a few days after I got in with Michelle and her little crowd.

It was like this: Mum wasn't letting me have the new clothes I wanted, so I decided to go and get them for myself. Michelle was always going on about how much she nicked and how easy it was. At the time I thought she was really cool about it, although, looking back, I think she just didn't care about getting caught. I really envied her, it just looked to me like a good way of getting what you want. She had the most fabulous gear, everything. I thought, Right, why not?

Since it was my first time we did a practice run nicking some make-up from the chemist's in Withington before we went out and tried some serious stuff — clothes down Manchester. Basically, you just have to think what people who nick things might look like, then look like someone else. The way Michelle told it, it was easy. You stroll into the shop, chatting away with your mate as though you're not really interested, you're just browsing, the stuff's not that good anyhow – then in the bag and out the door as soon as the shop assistants turn their backs. Easy! Except, I got spotted.

Funny thing is, I knew someone was watching me but I just kept hoping that if I went on and did it they'd take no notice. It was like I was on a machine that I couldn't stop. I could see this woman with her eyes on me the whole time but it was like, I wasn't going to back down, you know? Like, it would have been so uncool to have to walk out without taking anything. That's the thing about being cool – it's so stupid. You'd never get a dog worrying about being cool. Being cool means you can't think about anything because you're so bothered about how you look – even if it means getting caught shoplifting because you're ashamed to admit that you're not cool enough to look innocent!

In the end, I grabbed some eyeliner and made for the door. The girl at the till just by the door tried to get in my way but I brushed past her and I was out into the street in a second and legging it up the road. The woman from the pharmacy counter dashed out and shouted, 'Stop her!' behind my back, but of course no one did anything. Michelle was still in the shop. While I was pelting up the road, gibbering and scared out of my wits, she was standing there on her own in the shop, stuffing about fifty quid's-worth of make-up in her bag while the shopkeepers were at the door watching me.

171

'It was a good trick, you getting spotted and taking the heat off me,' she teased me after. She gave me half the stuff she'd had away and wanted to do it again straightaway.

'Yeah, no problem,' I said, as if the whole thing had been cool. We started planning our big trip into town but it was already too late. I'd been recognised as I legged it off down the road. The police were round at my place that same afternoon.

I was at the table with Mum when Adam came to the kitchen door.

'There's a police car outside and I think they're coming in here,' he said. Mum looked at me and the blood must have gone from my face because she knew at once.

'It's you, isn't it?' she said, and then the bell rang.

'That's them. What have you done?' asked Adam.

Mum was up and grabbed me by the arm. 'Come on, you, upstairs, come on,' she hissed.

'You're not going to hide her, are you? That's illegal!' said Adam, the little twat. He screwed up his face and chased after us. 'I don't want to live in a house with a criminal,' he bellowed.

'Shut up, keep your voice down!' hissed Mum. 'You answer the door, tell them she's not in,' she told him, hustling me upstairs.

'I'm not telling lies to the police!' shouted Adam.

'Shut up, they'll hear you,' I hissed.

'I'm not telling lies, I don't want to get arrested for

telling lies,' he yelled. 'If she's done something wrong she should go to jail, not me,' he ranted. I wish! Mum had me on the landing by this time. She shoved me into her room.

'In the wardrobe!' She pushed me in and closed the door and ran back downstairs. I could hear Adam booming away like some sort of burglar alarm so she sent him out into the back garden and answered the door herself. Me, I was standing in the wardrobe on a huge pile of her shoes wetting my knickers. I nearly did, really. I was terrified. I was thinking, I'm sorry, please don't let them find me, I'll be good. I heard voices downstairs. Then there were feet coming up the stairs, and I didn't know if it was Mum or them. The door opened – I nearly died – and it was Mum.

'Right, you, downstairs. What have you been up to? Nicking things from the chemist's, you stupid, stupid girl. Go on, down you go!' And she dragged me out and practically pushed me downstairs and got the whole story out of me, while Adam stood goggling in from the doorway.

'Is she going to jail? Is she going to jail?' he kept asking, and I kept shouting,

'Just piss off, will you, little freak!' and Mum was threatening me with every form of hell this earth has to offer. In the end she had a word with the chemist and got them to drop charges, but I had to go round and apologise in public and pay them back the fifty quid's-worth Michelle had away before they agreed to do it.

Mum was great. She even helped out with the money. Afterwards she wanted me to help do this car boot sale she was going to, but you know what? I was too selfish even to do that. I wasn't giving up my Saturday for her. I should have been turned into a cow rather than a dog, I was that bad.

You know, I'd forgotten all about that incident. I never think about anything, me, I just do it. I never look back or have regrets. Sometimes I think that I never even have any hopes for the future. That's why things got so bad between me and Mum for a while. I never thought about what I'd done, so all I'd be left with was the horrible feelings that I'd caused, and I'd think it was all Mum's fault, because it was with her that I was feeling so bad. But I can't help it. It's just me. It's just that the person she wants me to be isn't the way I am.

And now here she was, on my side again even though just about everything about me was different. Now there was the rest of the family to convince as well. Dad and Adam both thought Mum was having a nervous breakdown. You could tell it by their voices. After the police had gone, Dad came up close to the bedroom door and started talking to her as if she was a kid.

'Sue? It's OK, Sue, everything's all right. You can open the door now,' he said in this calm, quiet voice, as if he was trying to tempt the cat out of a cupboard.

'Have they gone?' demanded Mum. She was sitting on the bed with one arm around my neck. I was shaking from head to foot, whimpering and licking her face, and she was twisting her head this way and that to keep my wet tongue off her. She never liked dogs, my mum. She never liked Ed, either.

'Yes, it's all right, they've gone. You can come out now,' soothed Dad.

'Is Adam still there?' demanded my mum.

'He's downstairs.'

Mum looked down at me and scowled. 'Oh, Jesus. I must be going mad!' I was so terrified she'd suddenly decide the whole thing was a dream that I started muttering, 'No, no, it's me, Mum, it's me,' and she jumped up and screamed, 'Shit!'

'What is it? Are you all right?' demanded my dad.

'It's talking again!'

I hung my head. It? Hadn't I shown enough to be a she yet?

Mum looked down at me and smiled weakly. 'I'm going to let your father in, and you have to go over the same tricks you did for me, OK? Just do everything I tell you. And don't talk! It sounds – it sounds like – not very nice.' She patted me encouragingly on the head, and went to open the door. I was so scared I scuttled off the bed and cringed behind it, my tail tucked in between my legs. I heard Dad come into the room; he stank of fear.

'Come on, Sandra, come out. It's just your dad,' said Mum soothingly. I crept round the side of the bed, licking my lips and trying to wag my tail, but it was hard work. Then she called Adam up. They both looked so huge, towering above me on their hind legs!

Mum took a deep breath and off we went, same as before. She sent me all round the house doing my tricks to prove I was human.

'Turn round three times. Get up on the bed. Roll over once. Bark four times. Go and get your socks off the dresser, the red ones. Fetch me the scarf from the back of the chair that you always used to wear with your leather jacket.' And so on.

As I ran around the bedroom, performing these little jobs, you should have seen Dad and Adam's faces! Their mouths opened wider and wider and wider, until they looked like a pair of deep sea fish. It made me laugh, huf huf, and Adam got nervous and took a step back.

'Go and touch your last birthday present with your front paw.' That was my stereo system. 'Pull your favourite CD from the shelf. Which book did Adam give you last Christmas?' On and on she went. And what choice did Dad and Adam have? How could they not believe? At last, my dad got down on his haunches and looked at me, staring in my doggy face, trying to see something of the girl he knew in there.

'Sandra?' he croaked. I wagged my tail and went towards him, but he stood quickly back up.

'It's your daughter!' scolded my mother. 'Hug her! Make her feel better!'

Dad came down to me again and opened his arms and I crept up to him, but I could tell by the way he smelt that he still didn't believe. I thought, Mum loves me more than you do, but it wasn't really fair to think that.

It was just that she was better at believing stupid things than he was.

Then it was Adam's turn.

'Go on,' she urged. 'Give your sister a pat. Show her you're pleased to see her.'

I went up to Adam and held out a paw, but he just stood and stared. He looked truly appalled, appalled and disgusted, as if he was being asked to eat dog food or something.

'Adam . . .' began my mum. But he couldn't take it. He made a funny choking noise, shook his head, turned and ran out of the room.

'Adam! Come back!' shouted Mum after him. I barked, 'Adam!' But it was too late. The front door banged. My mum groaned, 'Oh, God,' and sat heavily down on the bed.

'Pretty difficult to accept,' said my dad. He walked over and sat down next to her. I stood in front of them, wagging my tail trustingly.

'What now?' said Mum.

Dad rubbed his chin. 'Perhaps a doctor?' he said. But something in his voice made me suspicious. Who did he want that doctor for? Me – or Mum? I think he still thought she'd gone completely round the twist.

EIGHT

I was back at home — not exactly in the bosom of my family, but still. I'd done it, and now I was exhausted. I crawled rather than walked to my bedroom. The door was shut, but I was too tired to be proud and I scratched to be let in like a dog. It was Dad who opened it for me. I gave him a grateful glance, and I'll never forget the look of distrust and amazement that he gave his little dog daughter as she slid back into the safety of her own bedroom. I jumped up on my bed, curled up and went straight to sleep.

I was woken up in the middle of my sleep by a strange, dream-like experience. In my exhausted state, still half asleep, it all seemed only half real.

The door opened. I remember thinking that I was dreaming. Adam came into the room. I was so much asleep that I couldn't even move my limbs. All I could do was lift up my head and open my eyes and watch. He stood over me, staring down and frowning as if the force of his frown could make him see me as I truly was, and although I knew this was what he was really trying to do, I had no idea why because I'd forgotten what had happened to me.

'You're not my sister,' said Adam slowly. He began to pace up and down in slow motion like a ghost made of flesh and blood.

'You're not my sister. You're horrible. My sister isn't horrible, she's beautiful. My sister's the most lovely girl anyone ever saw. Everyone thinks so. Everyone admires her and likes her. She knows how to live, she understands all about people. She's great. Sandra's great and you're just a stupid, stupid, little bitch.'

He stood there looking at me for a while longer before he left the room, closing the door quietly behind him. I put my head back down and went straight back to sleep. When I awoke, as I say, it felt like a dream because I was so tired, but I remembered everything about it, even the texture of the skin around his eyes, which had a grainy, strained look about it. What he said didn't hurt me, it touched me. It touched me so much it made me cry. You see, I never knew he felt like that about me. I thought I was just a pain in the neck to him, someone who got in the way, who probably stole too much of our mum's attention away from him with all my goings-on. To think, all the time he loved me, and looked up to me! It made me feel bad about all the times I'd thought I hated him. But at the same time, it made me feel depressed. It's just so hard, isn't it? All these different relationships – Mum, Dad, Adam, Simon, Annie. All these different people, all wanting different things. You can never get it all right, can you? People's lives – it's a wonder they don't burn themselves out and die before they ever grow up just trying to get along together. I was so dopey I only half realised what was going on, and I thought to myself, Thank God, at least I don't have to worry about any of that any more, before sleep closed up again over my head.

When I awoke properly I was feeling hungry. In fact, I was ravenous. I could have rushed downstairs to the kitchen and stuck my head in the rubbish bin, but I was sticking to my decision to behave myself, so I had to get dressed first. My knickers and little skirt had stayed downstairs and all I had on was a tee-shirt. Mum must have come in and tidied up while I was asleep, but she'd left out some clothes – an old pair of knickers that were too small – I mean, they used to be too small. They were about ten sizes too big, now. There were some little shorts out, too, which was a good idea, and a pair of ankle warmers – another good idea. I hesitated before putting them on – I wanted to choose my own clothes. It had been years since I'd let Mum tell me what to wear. But I didn't have time to be so proud, not any more.

I put the clothes on, left the room – and there were the stairs. No one was looking, so I quickly ran down on all fours. There was no point in making another noise falling down again.

The family were in the kitchen. They all turned to look at me when I came in, and it made me feel uncomfortable, being so far beneath them. I climbed up onto a kitchen chair and sat upright like a dog begging.

I wasn't begging though. I just wanted to be on the same height as the rest of them.

'Sandra?' said my mum haltingly.

I nodded my head and said, 'Yuf!'

'Sandra, Julie's coming round. I — we — haven't told her about, about what's happened to you. We've just told her that it's about you and that it's very important. She should be here, well, any minute now.'

So that was why they were all looking so nervous! I think we're all a little bit afraid of Julie. She's always so sure of herself and she has such clear ideas about things — you can't help feeling she knows what's going on, although she's told me before now that she doesn't know any better than anyone else, really. Inside, she's just as unsure of herself as the rest of us. That's what she says, anyway, but I think she just likes the idea of being modest and isn't really like that at all. I think she thinks she's right practically all the time.

What Mum said made my heart sink. We all relied on Julie for her common sense, her ability to look right into the heart of a situation. I was scared silly. Julie was far too level headed to believe in anything as impossible as me! She sees things very clearly, Julie, but she just hates it if you disagree with her, and I couldn't see her agreeing with this one.

First thing, though — I had to have some food inside me. I slid down off my chair and, using the sides of the table to help me stay upright, I walked on my hind legs to the fridge and tried to pull the door open with my paw. It was hard – my balance wasn't good enough. I looked over my shoulder. They were all staring at me with their mouths wide open. I thought, What are they all staring at? Haven't they ever seen anyone go to the fridge for food before? What did they think a fridge was for?

'I'm hungry!' I explained. Dad turned pale and Adam turned red. Mum's hand went back up to her mouth. It was making me feel cross, this permanent staring as if I was some sort of freak.

'I think she wants something to eat,' said Adam.

'What shall I give her?' asked Mum, and Adam said,

'We haven't got any – have we?'

'What?'

'Well, dog food.'

How dare he! But he just went on, 'I could ring Julie and ask her to get some on the way round.'

Mum had gone to the cupboard. 'I've got some tinned stew, do you think she'd like that?'

'If it's supposed to be Sandra . . .' began my dad.

'She,' snapped Mum. 'If *she's* supposed to be Sandra.'

'Sorry. If *she's* supposed to be Sandra, maybe she'd like what Sandra likes. Why not make her a fried egg sandwich?'

'Good idea,' said Mum, although I wasn't sure there wasn't a trace of sarcasm in Dad's voice. I certainly saw him and Adam exchange glances. But Mum did as he suggested. At last the sandwich was ready, but then, after being so good, Mum let me down badly by putting it on the floor. I wasn't having that. I jumped up onto a chair, and said, 'Up here, please!' although you wouldn't have guessed that's what I was saying by the noise I made.

Mum hesitated, then quietly cut the food up into small pieces before putting it down in front of me. I didn't make a fuss about that – she only did it so I wouldn't have to slobber and chomp over the big pieces of bread.

'Perhaps she'd like a knife and fork,' said Adam.

'Adam!' snapped Mum.

'Oh, sorry, right, you don't need a knife and fork for sandwiches, do you?'

'Adam, that's enough!'

'Well. If she's so human why can't she make her own sandwich?'

'Don't be stupid, she's doing her best. She can't – help herself very much at the moment. It's like I said – like she's disabled or something.' I caught a glance of Adam rolling his eyes at Dad. I thought, Well – I'll show them! Then I wolfed down my sandwich. It wasn't bad. I admit I'd have preferred meat but I'd rather have died than admit that to them. Then Mum made tea. She put mine in a wide pint mug, bless her, so I could lap out of it, and we all sat in an uncomfortable silence, and waited for Julie to arrive.

Ten minutes later there was the sound of a key in the front door.

'I hope she hasn't bought Angelo with her,' said Dad.

'Keep the family shame a secret,' said Adam. Then the kitchen door opened and in came Julie.

'What's that?' she asked as she came in, catching sight of me. 'You haven't gone and got a dog, have you?' she asked Mum. She reached down to pat me and I started licking her hand, but then I thought, No, that's not me – licking the hand of anyone who wants to pat me, so I stopped.

Mum stood up, ran her fingers through her hair and said, 'Watch.'

She made me do all the tricks all over again. First of all the dog ones, sit up, roll over, play dead, beg. Julie was laughing and clapping me on to start with. Then we got on to the slightly dodgy ones, a bit too clever for a dog – shake your right paw, shake your left paw, tap the ground five times, tap the ground thirteen-take-away-seven times. Julie's eyes started to pop out of her head. I was enjoying myself. Then Mum got on to the family ones – how old is Julie, how old is Adam? When she got to, tap out your birthday, I turned to face Julie as I did it. She didn't know who I was yet, she only knew that I was impossible. She was always saying that sort of thing to me. 'You're impossible, Sandra. Grow up!' You know. Now she was going to learn just how impossible I really was.

As I tapped out fourteen for the day, her face turned a chalky white. As I tapped out ten for the month, she backed off and leaned against the work surface, her hand groping at her mouth as if she'd forgotten what it was for.

'Tap out the year, then,' said Adam.

'Shut up, Adam,' said Mum. 'Just do the digits separately,' she told me. I did the one, pause; the nine, pause; the eight, pause, then three.

Julie let out a little moan. You could feel the temperature in the room drop.

Dad put his arm around her and led her a little further up the counter away from me. As far as he was concerned, I was something out of the Special Effects department.

'What's this all about?' demanded Julie. She pushed Dad's arms off her and looked around the room, at Mum, at Dad, at Adam – but not at me. No one said a word. 'What are you trying to tell me?' she asked, but no one had the courage to answer her. Dad and Adam looked down at their shoes. Mum chewed on a nail.

'You tell me,' she said.

'Are you trying to tell me...?' Julie paused and shook her head, because she didn't want to have to be the one who said it. But no one else was going to say it for her.

'How do you explain it?' demanded Mum. 'How can a dog do all those things? Just tell me that!'

'Are you trying to tell me that this...dog...this... dog...is...our Sandra? Is that it? Is that what you're trying to tell me?' Julie leaned forward.

Mum closed her eyes and nodded. She looked as if she'd just swallowed a fish whole.

'Mum.' Julie got off the worktop and walked up to

185

her. 'Mum!' She turned round at Dad. 'Have you been going along with this?'

'No one's going along with anything. How do you explain it then? Go on, explain it to me because there's only one answer I can see,' insisted Mum. I ran to her and leaned my back against her legs, but Julie had just got going.

'Look at it. It has four legs, teeth at one end, hair in the middle and an arsehole at the back. It's a dog. It craps on the pavement. People are different. You might have noticed. Two legs for instance. Flat faces, fingers, that sort of thing. Conversation. Remember?'

'I know what people look like, Julie.'

'It doesn't look anything like Sandra! Sandra hasn't got a big nose, Sandra hasn't got a two-foot tongue – it doesn't even have the same hair colour as Sandra, for God's sake!'

Adam had started giggling. I growled at him to shut up, and he shut up.

Mum was furious. 'Then how, how, how, how do you explain it?' she shouted.

'How should I know? How can I explain it? It's some sort of freak. It doesn't behave like a dog, but it *is* a dog, any idiot can see that. Give it to a vet, maybe they'll be able to find out what's wrong with it. Give it to the university, I don't know. It's probably a circus dog. They can train them to do anything. They can do anything with smells, dogs...'

'Smells won't help it count, Julie!'

'It can't count! It just reacts to certain words with a certain number of taps. I've seen horses do it. Dad?' Julie looked appealingly at him. Dad rubbed his face.

'How does it know all those things about the family?' he asked.

'She's been kidnapped, the kidnappers have trained it. Sandra gave them all that information and they trained it . . .'

'What, in four weeks?' asked Dad.

'Maybe they've been training it up for ages. Maybe four weeks is enough. How do I know how long it takes to train a dog?'

'But what *for*? Don't you think we've been through all this?' Dad demanded. 'Don't you think we've tried all the other explanations? The trouble is,' he said, 'the trouble is, no matter which way you look at it, it's impossible, that's what the trouble is. It just doesn't make sense.'

'People don't turn into animals!' insisted Julie.

'Dogs don't know the things people do,' said Dad.

'Werewolves,' said Adam suddenly. I might have known his contribution would be something barmy like that. 'Maybe she's a werewolf, or a weredog or something.'

Julie waved her hand at him. 'You've been watching too many crap films.'

'Well, you tell me what it is then, because you haven't so far. It's all very well looking for a rational explanation, but this isn't rational, is it? It's supernatural. She *must* be a werewolf.'

I was listening to this conversation with my heart

banging like a bullet inside me. Which way was it going to go? But suddenly I felt that I had to join in. I stood up. Everyone in the room looked at me and went quiet. It was difficult balancing. I was getting better at it but I still sort of tottered round in a circle. Then I managed to straighten myself up and looked Julie in the eye. I cleared my throat with a gruff little cough and said,

'Julie. Julie. It's me. I am Sandra.'

Julie went as white as a sheet. 'Why's it growling at me? Look out! It knows I haven't been taken in...I think it's turning savage!' As she spoke she backed off towards the fridge. I took a couple of steps after her and she screamed, 'Get it away from me!'

'She's trying to talk,' said Mum. 'She talks! Do you understand? She talks!'

'*Talks*? Have you all gone stark staring bonkers? It's a bloody dog, for God's sake, it doesn't talk, it growls! Get a grip, will you? I know, we're all under a strain, but, Jesus, I could do without this, I really could! Christ! D, O, G, dog! Dog! Dog!'

There was another pause. Mum had gone very pale. I looked pleadingly up at her, but I could see that Julie had shaken her conviction that I was her daughter.

'You heard it talk, didn't you, Adam?' she asked. 'It said Adam, didn't it?'

Adam licked his lips. 'It sounded a bit like Adam but that doesn't mean anything. There was that dog on telly that used to say sausages, remember that? No one said that was a person, did they?'

Julie edged around me and put her arm around Mum's shoulders. 'Mum, I know how much you miss her. I miss her too. But this isn't going to bring her back! You're just stretching out the agony. Really! That dog is not your daughter. You can see that, can't you?'

Mum looked at me with wild eyes, then suddenly burst into tears and buried her face in Julie's shoulder. I just stared in horror. Things had been going so well, but now they were all turning against me. Julie patted Mum's shoulder and went on, 'What we need to do is call the police so they can find out who's done this. One thing *is* true – this dog is evidence that Sandra's still alive. If someone's gone to all this trouble to train a dog to know things only she knows, it probably means she's . . . well, that she's still alive. You see? OK, Mum?'

Mum had a tissue up to her face, but she nodded.

'You'll call the police, Mum?'

Mum paused and shook her head. 'I'll think about what you've said. Just – give me a little time to get used to the idea. I don't want to – that is, I can't hand her over yet.'

She looked down at me as she spoke, and she looked just devastated. I was looking from Mum to Adam to Dad to Julie, but none of them could meet my eye. I'd come so far and now they were going to give me up, send me to the police and God knows what sort of fate. With a howl of disappointment I turned and fled the room, ran up to my bedroom and flung myself on the bed to cry my heart out. A minute later, I heard someone creep up outside and start fiddling at the door – jamming the handle somehow. I was trapped, but I didn't care. Tears were streaming down my face. Julie didn't want me, Adam didn't want me, Dad didn't want me. All that I could have put up with, but now even Mum was turning her back on me. All I wanted to do was die, as soon as possible, and put an end to my miserable, useless life. But even as I thought that, as I lay there at the bottom of despair, I knew I wasn't going to die. I'd never give up, I'm not that sort. Girl or dog, I was going to carry on being myself right up until my last breath, no matter how bitter it was to do it.

And when I thought that, instead of feeling sorry for myself, I was taken over by a terrible rage. I mean, who did they think they were? What right did they have to decide who I bloody was? It was the same story all over again – all people ever want to do is to judge you. If you don't look right, you're wrong; if you don't behave right, you're wrong, no one wants to know you. It doesn't make any difference how much you need them or how much you love them, or how much they love you. If you don't fit – out! You're a slut, you're no good, you're worth nothing! Out! Out!

When I'd been working hard at school and had friends like Annie and a nice boyfriend like Simon, then I was the lovely daughter. But because I'd dropped Annie and started seeing other people, people who had a bit of life in them, because I started seeing other boys, suddenly I was no good, no one liked me, everyone thought I was just some little piece of shit stuck to their heel. Now I was a dog and it was just exactly the same. So what was so bad about being a dog anyway? Human beings think they're it, they really do – but they're not it, I can tell you! I've tasted life from both sides and I can tell you – worry worry worry, stress stress stress. Don't do this, do that, think this, how dare you – it's just a long stupid game with more and more stupid rules to take up your precious time.

I ran around my bedroom, champing my jaws and snarling and growling. Can you blame me? So I was a dog! So what? It was still me inside, if only they took the trouble to know me. But oh, no – they knew better! They knew exactly what I was!

At least as a dog you knew where you were. At least you could trust your friends. At least people didn't let you down! The more I thought about it, the more my life as a dog seemed better than my life as a person. Fella loved me. Mitch did, too – they'd both have died for me if they had to and they'd never judged me once in all the time I'd known them. See Mum and Dad or Adam or Julie doing that! Or Simon, or Annie, or Michelle or Wayne or Dobby, or Mosley, the guy I took home from Swingler's that night, or Dave or Jason, or any of those other lads I'd been with over the past year. In fact, life as a dog was pretty bloody good. Not with Terry – sod him – but running with the pack, hunting, using my nose and my wits to stay alive! What could be better than that? A dog's life burns bright when she's not sold out to some master or mistress. Short, but oh, so sweet. And here I was about to throw all that away!

I began to remember how pissed off I'd been with seeing Simon every weekend, doing my homework so neatly every night, helping around the house, all that shit. Now I could just do what I wanted and where was I? Out with the pack? No, I was stuck here at home weeping and wailing because my bloody family couldn't accept me as I was. So what's new? What had changed? Nothing – not even myself, when it came down to it.

I was so furious I hardly knew what I was doing. I raged around the bedroom, leaping up and tearing the cushions and sheets with my teeth, I was so upset. I chewed my school books – no more bloody work for me! I pulled the duvet off the bed, I peed on the carpet, I shook my clothes until the stitches popped. I thought my rage would go on forever, but then, as I was nosing about looking for something else to attack, I found Mr Brown, my old teddy I've had since I was three. He was lying half buried under a pile of shredded clothes. I didn't have the heart to tear him to pieces. Instead, I picked him up tenderly in my jaws and carried him to my bed. I held him in my legs, licked his face, and gradually began to calm down and think properly.

I was never much good at being a person, me. It's so hard! It's hard, it's hard, being a person. I lay there on that bed and I thought, God, this is going to go on for another seventy years! Seventy years of people pushing you into being something you're not. Seventy years of rage and anxiety, worrying about things you don't care about, like GCSEs and if you're dressed nicely and if your face is clean and if you're making your mum or your husband or your kids unhappy and whose feelings you're going to hurt next. Seventy years of getting up in the morning when you don't want to and going somewhere you don't like. Tests and rules and skills and assessments, and then another set of tests and rules and skills and assessments. On and on and on and on and on it goes. What's the point? Why bother? I wasn't ambitious, I wasn't going to change the world. All I wanted was to have a good time. I mean!

There were things I missed. My parents, my friends. Oh, I know I moan about them but that doesn't mean I don't love them. And the dances and the music, the whole thing. Packets of crisps, clothes, money in your pocket. People! I love people. There's a hundred great things about being a human being. I thought about how I used to look, my slim legs and my smooth tummy, my round breasts with their pretty pink nipples and my smiley face, and how much I missed looking like me . . . but then there was Fella sniffing under my tail and growling to himself, 'Hmmm, that's good!' That made me lick my lips. I looked up and caught sight of myself in the mirror and waggled my eyebrows up and down, and the sight of a dog waggling her eyebrows was so funny I laughed, Huf huf huf!

I felt better then. I curled up and tucked my nose under my tail so I could breathe in my sweet scents, and fell asleep lying there on the bed, breathing in the rich centre of my dogginess.

I've no idea how long I lay there. I knew I was being unfair — as if they could know me just like that! But it was very hard to forgive them, especially Mum, for doubting me after all my efforts to be human again. I kept dozing and dreaming and coming to, and trying to make sense of it. I'd nuzzle up to Mr Brown and then doze off again. I didn't wake up properly until the door rattled and opened, and there was Mum staring at me with a face like cracked glass.

'Oh, you bad dog!' she cried. She ran into the room. I backed off on the bed, half wagging my tail. What had I done? 'Look at the state of this room! Look at it — it's wrecked!' I looked around. It was a tip. I'd chewed it half to pieces. Then she caught sight of Mr Brown lying on the bed and she went ballistic.

'Look what you've done! Oh, how could you, you bad dog, you've chewed her teddy to pieces! Just look at it! Oh, you bad, bad dog!' She reached forward and snatched him off the bed in front of me and waved him in my face. It was true! Mr Brown was in tatters, his stuffing leaking out all over the place, his head all soggy. I must have been chewing him in my sleep. I let out a whimper of surprise, but Mum was livid.

'BAD dog! BAD dog!' she yelled. 'Look at it, it's

ruined. What will Sandra say, letting a bad dog like that sleep in her room and put on her clothes and chew up her teddy? Well, now I KNOW you're not my Sandra! Sandra would never treat her things like this, she always loved that bear, how could you do such a thing! Oh, now we see your true colours...' On and on she went, holding the bear to her breast and shouting and weeping. I could hardly believe my ears. I don't know why she'd picked on Mr Brown when the rest of my room was all chewed up. I'd never even liked Mr Brown! It was the first time I could ever remember taking him to bed, I'd only done it now because he reminded me of the past.

On the stairs feet came pounding. Dad and Adam were on their way up to see what the fuss was about.

'Look! She's chewed Sandra's things to pieces. Look at her teddy!'

'I told you, I told you it wasn't her!' shouted Adam.

'That proves it!' yelled my dad. All three of them started shouting and blaming each other and yelling how obvious it was that I wasn't Sandra, and how they'd never really believed it at all, and how could they have been so stupid as to be taken in by such a ridiculous dog, and on and on and on...

I couldn't believe it! It was as if all the time they'd just been waiting for me to make one tiny little mistake so they could turn against me! It was so typical! Just like it used to be, just so like the way they always behaved towards me. All they ever wanted was the slightest excuse to turn on me. It made me so angry that it was never enough for me to be myself. Oh, no, I had to be so *good* as well, so bloody good, and if I wasn't good enough then I was out on my bloody ear. Call the police! Get her put down! Kill her! She's chewed up her teddy!

Well, it was my teddy, wasn't it? I could do what I wanted to my own teddy. With a snarl I leaped off the bed and seized Mr Brown in my jaws, tearing him from Mum's grasp. I landed in the middle of the room right in front of them, daring them to try and take him off me. Mum shrieked, 'Stop it! Stop it!' and reached forward, but I growled so fiercely that she didn't dare try.

'GRRRRRRRRRR!' I told them, and I began to rip that bear to shreds, shaking my head until the stuffing flew, pawing at it, getting it down on the ground and biting savagely at its head. My family were terrified – they couldn't get out of that room fast enough! They were yelling, 'MAD DOG!' and falling all over each other and clawing at each other to try and get out of the room first. The air was a blizzard of stuffing. Then the door slammed. And you know what? I was laughing my head off. If only they'd known, half my growls were snorts of laughter. I mean! Mad dog! Oh God, she's got rabies! Mad dog! And why? Because I was chewing my teddy? I mean, is that it? How ridiculous can you get!

But I wasn't laughing for long.

'It's gone mad!' yelled Dad.

'Just like last time!' howled Adam.

'That's it, I've seen enough,' yelled Mum. 'Get the police, let's get rid of it once and for all!'

I heard them fumble with the door handle, jamming it up again. I couldn't believe my ears. Where they really going to murder me for chewing up my teddy bear? Once again I was staring the dog pound in the face. It's like I've spent half the last year, girl and bitch, being threatened. Experiments. Tests. Just because you're an animal they think you don't have any basic rights. Human rights, that's what they call them, don't they?

I ran to the window and looked out. It was open an inch at the bottom, enough to let a little air circulate – my mum always hated the smell of dogs. I put my nose underneath and began to work it up, and as I did it there was a noise in the garden below me. Two dogs jumped out of the hedge and walked proudly onto the lawn below me. Fella and Mitch! They'd been out there all the time!

'We've been waiting for you!' barked Mitch. He and Fella walked forward into the garden, tails high, wagging slowly from the pleasure of seeing me again. I felt my heart leap inside me. What was I doing here, in this house, with these people? Surely, certainly, I was a dog, and here was my own kind waiting to welcome me!

'It's not too late,' barked Fella. 'Oh, you pretty little bitch! Come to me, baby! Jump!'

'Jump! Jump! Jump! Jump!' barked Mitch over and over again. He was so excited he started to jump up and down himself, making little whiny noises. I pushed my nose right under the window and with a good hard shove got it up far enough to wriggle out. But I hesitated. I was certain that if I left again I'd never come back. Was I ready for that?

'You're not one of them!' yelped Fella. 'You can't trust them, they don't know how to have fun, they don't even know who they are half the time! Jump, baby! Come on, jump!'

'You've got nothing to lose – you've already lost it!' barked Mitch. 'Remember the taste of rabbit blood on your tongue! The pack at night, the grass under your paws, your tireless feet!'

'Remember the time we had in the Southern Cemetery!' barked Fella. 'Remember the cats. We still gotta catch a cat! The smells on the pavement and lamp-posts, the freedom to go where you like and sleep when you want! What are you waiting for? Jump!'

I gathered my strength beneath me. What was I waiting for? I thought, Jump, jump, you silly bitch! I could hear my family shouting downstairs, terrified at the sights and sounds that were going on. Fella being Fella, he was barking away in a variety of accents – Welsh, Irish and Caribbean.

I could hear my mum saying in a stunned voice, 'Is that dog barking in Welsh? Is that dog barking in Welsh?' Then Adam started screaming again – the idiots.

'What are you waiting for?' pleaded Fella. 'You and me, baby! We'll feast on cats! We're a new breed, baby. Come on! There's nothing for you there.'

I think my whole life – not my life that had gone, but my life to come – flashed before my eyes. Back to school, working away like mad to get exams I wasn't going to do well at, so I could get a crap job in a crap company with long hours that'd inch by inch by inch turn me into everybody else. Work work work, every day learning how to be good at something I wasn't good at, doing things I didn't want to do, living for weekends and three weeks' holiday a year. Parenthood! Sweating and straining to pop out a fat helpless baby; worry and care and stress. Never having enough money to do anything you want to do, and only just enough to do what you have to. Coming home to the baby and doing more work, and then making the baby turn into everybody else as well. Years and years and years of it. Nappies and shit and exams and tests and work and forever and ever and ever amen.

Then I thought about being a dog under the night sky with the dew in her coat, who spills her puppies out and mourns without despair. Her life isn't worry and work, it's loyalty and blood, fear and love – the brief passion for yet another dog on your back, yet another batch of puppies to love and to throw away. Life and death seized between your jaws; mating, hunting and then to die in a splash of blood under the wheels of a lorry. And I thought, I don't want to be a human being. I never was a human being in the first place. I want to be quick and fast and happy and then dead. I don't want to grow old. I don't want to go to work. I don't want to be responsible. I want to be a dog!

'Jump!' barked Mitch. 'Jump! Jump! Jump!'

'Jump! Jump!' barked Fella.

There were feet behind me on the stairs, the door burst open. Mum ran in.

'Don't go!' she cried.

'Let her go!' shouted Adam from downstairs.

My legs gathered under me. The window was open. I jumped.